MW01644637

Producer & International Distributor
eBookPro Publishing
www.ebook-pro.com

THAT TIME I DIED

Naomi Peled Schneider

Translation: Noam Heller

Contact: naomipeled751@gmail.com

ISBN 9798858637332

That Time I Died

Naomi Peled Schneider

1.

I lie in a bed, in a white room that smells of antiseptic. The strong smell blankets the room, forcing me back into reality. It's a shame, because I was just now in New York, strolling the streets and taking in the cool winter air. It seemed like I'd arrived just before Christmas. A blanket of snow covered the city streets, and I could hear the crunch of the snow as I wandered around Fifth Avenue. Thousands of people poured into the stores looking for the perfect Christmas gifts, and yellow, festive lights dangled in the streets, illuminating the whole street.

In truth, it didn't surprise me that I'd escaped to New York for a while. I do this quite often—vanish, fade away, and disappear for several hours. I choose a new destination each time, leaving my body behind as I escape. I really love the feeling I get when I arrive at a new place. In a matter of seconds, I immerse myself in the novel scenery, with its unique scents and unfamiliar tastes. I become so engrossed that I completely forget myself. It's only when I drift off like that that I can forget everything. Only when I float somewhere else can I forget this dreary hospital, this bulky metal bed I've been chained to for so long.

I hear footsteps approaching the door and instantly shut my eyes. Yeah, I pretend to be asleep sometimes. And yeah, it took me a while, but today, I can confidently say that I'm an expert at detecting footsteps, to the point where I know who's about to enter the room.

It's this guessing game I've been playing with myself to avoid going nuts.

It was Fanny, the nurse. I can distinguish her swift, small footsteps, and the smell of her sweet perfume, the one she douses herself with. She entered the room and immediately began organizing my bed. Even though my eyes were shut, I could sense she was glaring at me. Fanny is the only one in the entire department who treats me like a real person, like a normal human being. That makes her different than everyone else here—she's authentic. Other people put on a "business as usual" front, but I can tell it's fake, just an act they're putting on for me. Deep down, I know they feel sorry for me. I know they're thinking to themselves, "Wow, poor Yair, look at what he did to himself."

At times I wish I was sick with some mysterious illness, some rare syndrome that affects one out of a million. If that were the case, I could easily join the "pitying choir" and pity myself with all the rest. I could feel sorry for my situation, and, of course, blame it all on fate. Cruel, cruel fate... how convenient it is to blame that abstract entity. The problem is, in my case, I'm the only one to blame for my horrible state, the responsibility is all mine. It's because of me that I'm lying in this bleak hospital bed.

Whenever I replay the final moments before the crash, I recall the thoughts that went through my mind: "Get off, you're crazy. You can die." I brushed them off like dust.

See, when you're seventeen, you have a special "idiocy pill" running through your veins, convincing you that you're invincible, unique, that the whole world is at your feet. Now that you're here, the world can relax. You feel like everything is under your control, and that you have nothing to worry about.

I remember seeing my friends standing on the hill, waiting for me to pull off my reckless "anaconda" trick. Everyone knew exactly what I was about to do, yet no one put in the effort to truly stop me. Well, as I said before, we were seventeen, high on our "idiocy pills," carefree, and certain that the whole world was waiting for us...

None of my friends dared to pull off such a radical move with the bike, which included speeding across a dirt road and flying in mid-air from one hill to the next, a menacing abyss separating both peaks stretching tens of feet long. We used to laugh about putting an end to life's miseries by doing the "anaconda." It seemed like a pretty solid way to go. We would also crack jokes if someone fell off their dirt bike and rolled on the ground, saying, "Going full anaconda, huh?" Just our usual way of making fun of each other's wipeouts.

"What have I done? What have I done?" I repeatedly asked myself as I hovered mid-air between both hills. In those few seconds spent above the ground, the magnitude of what I'd done hit me like a brick wall. I was obviously far away from the second hill, and I had no chance whatsoever of making it. I was diving headfirst into the abyss.

I was in the air for only about three seconds or so, but my mind whirled with endless thoughts. It's crazy how many thoughts can race through my mind in a matter of seconds, far quicker than the time it takes me to act. Thoughts of death, fear, thoughts preparing me for the crash, and thoughts of it all ending.

"Daily checkup," Fanny, the nurse, announced.

"Anything new since yesterday?" I muttered under my breath and kept my eyes closed.

"Where are you hanging out today? Are you riding your bike? Surfing? Skydiving?" she asked.

My eyelids stayed shut, even though I knew she was smiling my way. I love how real she is. And while some may call her rude, I know she's just trying to brighten up this gray place, that's all. I'd take her bold attitude any day over everyone else's politeness and ridiculous small talk about the weather... as if I could care less.

"It's too windy to go surfing, don't you think? The forecast said there's a storm coming, oh, wait... what am I talking about." She laughed. "This is just the right weather for you surfers, isn't it? You guys are just dying for days like these to ride monster waves, aren't you?" She paused whatever she was doing to hear my answer.

When I didn't budge, she continued, "Just don't forget to invite me to the beach, I'll come to watch you surf, I promise." She released the blood pressure cuff from my upper arm and placed her stuff back into the cart.

"I don't really like strong winds, especially when I'm near the beach. It's always so cold, brr... but no worries, I'll sit in the car with a cup of tea and watch you tear down those waves. Deal?"

She hovered a few inches above my face in the hopes of getting a response. She succeeded. I couldn't handle it anymore so I let out a smile but kept my eyes shut.

"Ah! Thank you!" she rejoiced and pinched my cheek. "You're truly something."

She covered me with a wool blanket and tucked me in tightly, like she was wrapping a present. "I'm leaving. Don't you forget to invite me, huh?" She spoke so casually that it almost felt like I was really about to hop out of bed, grab a surfboard and head out to sea. She turned to the door and said goodbye, her Latin accent rolling off her tongue playfully.

That's it. I'd lost my desire to travel around New York and decided to float to my dad's lab instead, back to the night of the crash. My dad doesn't know I was there that night, he doesn't know that I heard what I heard, that I crawled into his lab and hid there. At times, I find it wild that I entered the lab as one person, and left as another. I spent only a few hours inside, but by the time I walked out, I was a completely different "Yair."

There are times when I feel bad for what I did, for those moments in the lab that changed me as a person. I'm not the same "Yair" who used to quietly sneak into this dad's lab and frighten him, a game we used to play to see who could scare who better. A game I usually won... just saying.

One late night, my Aunt Esther, who found religion a few years ago, dropped by for a visit, and I, of course, pretended to be asleep. Each time she comes, she prays to G-d. In a way, I'm jealous of her faith, of how confident she is that there's some entity listening to her on the other side of the call. The moment she stepped into my room, she took out a small Book of Psalms and began to pray earnestly.

A few moments later, she rested her head on my blanket and whispered, "God almighty, watch over this child, he's pure, he's a good soul. Please, have mercy on him. He has his whole life ahead of him. Even if he made a mistake, forgive him. Have mercy on his family. Save him, save us. I beg of you." Her voice trembled. It was clear that she meant every word she said.

Looking back, I don't recall speaking to G-d more than once in my life. Like most idiots, I cried out for help only when my life was at a huge risk. In my case, it happened on the beach when I crashed into a boulder and nearly drowned. Yeah, like most self-centered beings, I called him only when I had no other choice, only when I was in dire need of help. Turns out, most people talk to G-d only when they're in big trouble.

My Aunt Esther taught me that I could also ask for help. If she could call him whenever she wanted, to talk about the smallest of things, as if he was right here in the room with her, then so could I. There's no reason for me not to be as close to him, I mean, I deserve a direct phone line as much as the next guy. And honestly, something has changed since I made the switch. Our conversations have changed immensely. We've progressed from having poor reception to long and satisfying conversations in which we talk about everything. Yes, we talk. I talk to him, and he answers me. I'm dead honest.

In the beginning, I thought I'd pray to him, just like my Aunt Esther does, and that would be that. But gradually, I realized that someone on the other end of the line was really picking up, as if he was right here in the room with me. I was sure I was imagining at first, but the longer our conversations lasted, the more I understood that this was real, that someone on the other end of the line was really talking to me.

I don't try to get anything specific out of our conversations. All I want is to talk, simply talk. Unlike Aunt Esther who treats him as a father, I treat him as a close friend, it feels more... right. There's a reason I call him "bro," it's a nickname I feel suits him.

On one hand, he's a straightforward guy who doesn't take it easy on me and says it like it is, and on the other, I feel extremely close to him. He's like the brother I never had.

It's weird, but in my life before the crash, despite being surrounded by friends and family, I always felt a bit lonely, and now, stuck here in this hospital on my own without many people around, I don't feel that way. I know he's here, by my side, at all times.

He always picks up the second I call him. Still... I admit that doubts may creep up at times. Is this really him talking? Why would he talk with me? I'm not that important. Why would he waste his time on me when there are so many other interesting and smart people in this world... and if he's not the one talking to me, then who is? Maybe whoever's talking with me is just a messenger, a spirit, or maybe—and this is a terrifying thought—it's all in my head, and I'm the one talking to myself. In truth, everything seems possible. I genuinely have no proof that G-d is the one picking up my calls.

For the longest time, I let doubts eat away at my mind to the point where I really felt like I was losing it. "Is it him, or is it not?" I asked myself over and over again, trapped in a vicious cycle of looping thoughts. Gradually, I noticed that the more I messed around with these questions, the shorter our conversations became. One day, I grew sick of it all and decided that enough was enough. I promised to stop questioning it and to simply enjoy our talks, without looking into whether it was him or not. Deep down, I know it doesn't matter. What matters is that someone is here talking with me and that I'm not alone. Who is doing the talking? I honestly don't care anymore.

Since I began having these conversations with G-d, I've slowly begun to understand what happened to me that day, why I decided to pull off the "anaconda" trick in the first place and dive head first into that impossible stunt. People normally don't try to understand why bad things happen to them. Good things can happen every day, all the time, and no one will question it, because it's supposedly a "given." People feel like they deserve good things in life. But if bad things happen, they get terribly upset. They blame everyone else but themselves and expect G-d to sort things out for them.

I, for one, am actually eager to try to understand why such a horrible thing happened to me, why this crash turned my life upside down. In fact, I already have a few ideas. It would be foolish to think that my crash happened by chance. I'm not a guy who believes in random chance.

2.

My mom entered the room and swiftly approached the side of my bed, a warm smile on her face. She began ruffling my blanket and straightening out my pillow, scanning my body as she always does. It seems like she's always surprised to see me in a vegetative state. Maybe because she thought I'd be better by now, but it's been months since the crash, and nothing has changed. Despite the time that has passed, she still hasn't gotten over it. She's always looking for signs of movement. Really, all she needs is one small twitch, one meager signal from my paralyzed body to prove to everyone that she was right and that this paralysis wasn't anything too major and I'd be back on my feet in no time, just like she said I would.

"How are you?" she seemed concerned.

"Great, just got back from the beach." I smiled lazily.

"Come on, enough with the cynicism. It's not going to help you get any better." She sounded impatient.

"Just to remind you, Mom, I'm not sick," I replied. She sat on the chair by my bed and drew her face closer to mine.

"How are you?" She seemed concerned.

"How am I?" I asked, unsure how to respond.

"Did you do what I asked?" Her voice was stern.

"What?" I replied.

"The guided meditation," she explained.

"Mom, enough, really. Enough with this nonsense. I don't believe in it, period, okay?!" I snapped back.

"Please, just try," she urged.

"No, I'm not interested." I was determined.

She took out a bottle of orange juice from her purse, poked it with a straw, and drew it near my mouth. "Why don't you try? Just try and picture yourself walking a few times a day, what is there to lose?" She placed the straw in my mouth.

"I'm not interested. Ugh, now my head hurts." I slowly slipped on the cold, tart juice.

"You can ask the nurse for a painkiller."

"Fine," I replied flatly.

"Come on, you're suffering for no good reason, drink some more." She poked my lips.

"Ahhh..." I sighed. "This thing is great" I lowered my voice to mimic an old man. "The little things in life, you know?" I rejoiced and mom laughed. "What about you? Don't you want some?" I raised a brow, but she shook her head. I looked at her dry lips. I could tell she hadn't had anything to drink since the morning. She always does this—rush over first thing in the morning before anything else.

The door of my room opened, and Dr. Sweed stepped inside. Mom quickly got up from her chair. In an instant, her face grew long and serious, and she curled her fingers around the metal bars of the bed for stability.

"Good morning." She smiled.

"Good morning," he replied dryly.

Dr. Sweed is not only the medical director of the department, but he's also the head surgeon, and in all of my months here in the hospital, I have never once seen him smile. He always wears a cold look on his face, as if to scare off anyone who might mistake him for an ordinary doctor and bother him with petty questions. I, for one, can't stand his attitude. I'm just an eighteen-year-old kid who up until a while ago was interested in: who won the soccer champion's league, whether the waves were fit for surfing, or if Talila was going to sleep over at my place. In truth, I've already come to terms with the fact that Dr. Sweed doesn't really care for the person he's treating. It seems like he doesn't care much for us. He's only here to save my paralyzed body. My dysfunctional body is his own private lab, where he busies himself trying to mend the broken pieces, and fix what's been destroyed. My vertebras, bones, skeleton, and blood vessels are all pawns in Dr. Sweed's game, and the truth of the matter is—the fact that they all belong to a person named "Yair," doesn't really interest him.

"Last week's surgery failed," Dr. Sweed stated without lifting his head from the medical file.

My mom's smile, which, up until now, had managed to put up with Dr. Sweed's freezing cold demeanor, was now wiped off her face. She leaned on my bed to prevent herself from collapsing.

"Why?" she faintly asked.

Dr. Sweed ignored her and went on, "We have another idea. When Dr. Bloch comes back from his trip abroad, we'll decide whether to operate again. And we're thinking of bringing in a medical expert from New York."

Silence lingered in the room. Dr. Sweed returned the

medical file to its place, and Mom remained stunned as ever, struggling to process the news.

"Where's your husband?" Dr. Sweed asked. For a moment, the doctor managed to surprise me. Could there be a bit of humanity left in him after all?

"He's away, coming back today... he flew to a conference," she stuttered with confusion, grabbed the orange juice, and slurped until the last drop. "So you're suggesting we wait for..." She managed to put together a few words, but Dr. Sweed carelessly cut her off as a reminder of how she was boring him to death with her questions.

"I'll update you later on." He turned around and headed toward the door.

"Thanks..." my mom whispered under her breath.

"Goodbye," he replied and stepped out.

The whole time Dr. Sweed was in the room, he hadn't looked at me once. I guess somewhere along his career, he simply lost that human connection, or maybe he never had it in the first place... maybe getting to know his patients is too much for him. In truth, as much as I find his behavior harsh, I get it. At least he's true to himself, behaving exactly as he wants to. I've always hated hypocrites. I see hypocrisy all around, and it drives me nuts, especially when it happens during visits. People come in, talk, smile, and laugh, but I know that the second they leave the room, they spit out what's really been racing through their minds the whole time. They surely complain about how hard it is to look at me, lying in bed, paralyzed, and cry over the monstrosity of my fate. What I find the worse, though, is when my parents are blamed for my situation, as if they're the ones responsible. I hate hearing people complain about how irresponsible my parents were for not knowing about our extreme tricks in the dunes. This Is obviously not true, they knew about what we were doing, and counted on me to be careful. My friends and I have always been cautious. Yeah, we enjoyed doing extreme stunts with our dirt bikes, but we always thought things through and made sure never to cross a line we couldn't bounce back from. My parents knew what we were doing in the nearby dunes. They trusted us, they knew they could. Only that, in my case, something unexpected happened, something that turned my life upside down, and turned me—from a responsible kid to a reckless one.

There's no way around it, I'm responsible! I truly am. And not due to recklessness, or because my parents hadn't educated me the right way, or because I had given in to peer pressure. I brought this upon myself because I was mad, because I couldn't believe what I heard in my dad's lab when I hid there under the desk. In those fateful moments, the anger boiled up in my body, took over, and tossed me to the darkest of places. I brought this upon myself. That's the truth—the cold hard truth.

My mom and I were left alone in the room. After a few moments of silence, my mom sat in front of the cabinet near my bed and began taking out all the stuff to wipe the shelves clean. There wasn't much need for it, obviously, but that's how she is, always cleaning things whenever she gets nervous. I knew she had high hopes for this last surgery, and now that it failed, the despair she was feeling was unbearable. I looked at her as she cleaned and organized my cabinet. I thought of saying something, but in those moments, I knew that the best thing to do was keep quiet and let the "cleaning therapy" soothe her. When she finished, she sat on my bed, and we spoke again.

"I think you missed a spot," I said.

"Where?" She jumped and scanned the cabinet through and through. I laughed. "Oh, enough with that!" She smiled and turned to me. "What will I do with you, kiddo? You're sweet and bitter like a piece of chocolate." She pinched my cheek and kissed my forehead.

"What *will* you do with me?" I asked, and the two of us lingered in silence, each one caught up in our own head.

"Well, I think I'll go to work," she said and forced herself up, grabbing her purse and pressing the cabinet closer to my bed.

"Yeah, you better go, I'm busy anyhow. Just about to head to the beach. I'm praying for some good wind today!" I said in all seriousness.

Mom laughed and stood by the door. "Okay, I'm going." She smiled and waved goodbye.

"I'd be happy to wave back, your highness, but I'm busy scratching my nose."

We both let out a final laugh.

Finally, after a moment of stillness, she turned around and left.

Honestly, I'm not as bitter or cynical as she pointed out. I'm really not. We've developed this sort of back-and-forth interaction as a way of not falling into despair. From the moment I crashed, my mom decided on a certain strategy, "business as usual," and I, with no other choice, must play along. I have to be there for her. After all, she's the person I love the most in this whole world, and if this is what will help her, then I will do it again and again and again. As much as needed.

We both knew that she wasn't going straight to work yet.

She was probably in the bathroom at the end of the hall, crying in one of the stalls. Crying about my shitty situation, about another failed surgery, and about dad being abroad when she needs him the most.

After this intense morning, I decided I needed to let off some steam and escape. This time, to the beach. I walked down to the beach, and let the warm wind stroke my face and the toasty sun wash over me. I could smell the salty air coming from the water, and inhaled it deeply into my lungs. I gave in to the golden rays, and when I felt like the scorching heat had roasted my skin enough, I picked up the surfboard and ran to the sea. That moment, crossing over from the sweltering heat to the freezing water always gives me pleasant goosebumps. The cool sprays of the sea on my body refresh my warm skin, and the blend of heat and cold brings my senses to life. I feel the closest to my truest self when I'm in the sea. I feel at home.

Ever since the crash, I began looking outward, and realized how blind I was to everything that didn't have to do with surfing. Before the crash, surfing was my whole life. The only reason I'd hop out of bed and go to school was to rush to the beach right after. The tall waves and strong winds were the only things that interested me. I would finish school, grab a quick bite, and run to the shore. A day without surfing seemed like a waste. Today, I can admit that I was completely addicted to the whole thing. Surfing was everything to me. I felt like I needed to ride waves all the time. I surfed every day, even if the weather showed that there wouldn't be wind. It didn't matter to me, I'd jump in the water anyway. Now, from the stiffness of this dreary bed in this gray hospital, I can see how addicted I was, how oblivious I was to anything other than surfing. Unbelievable really, like a horse with a patch on its eye, preventing it from looking sideways; that's how I was.

In the afternoon, just as I stepped out of the water to the cool air in search of a towel, my dad entered the hospital room. In my mind, I was still looking for a towel and eventually chose to sit on the soft sand instead, tilting my head back and letting the sun rays melt onto my skin. It's only when I'm nature that I feel this free. In these moments, I realize that I'm the only thing there is. Only what I choose to feel, see, hear, taste, and smell, will become part of my reality. Apart from my senses, apart from these bodily "windows" glimpsing outward, everything else is covered in darkness, nonexistent. It's only me living inside this body, just like everyone else is in theirs. My ability to picture myself anywhere else saves me. Without these escapes, I'm not sure I would've been able to survive this. It always surprises me how easily I can float away from the hospital and be elsewhere. There's a thin line between our reality and our imagination, between what's here and what's there. The boundary separating my imagination and reality grows blurry, to the point where, at times, I can confuse what's here in this room with what's out there. I can confuse my physical disability with health, and nature with this constricted room.

Normally, my mom is the only person I'm willing to open my eyes and snap back into the room for, but my dad was standing pretty close to my bed, and he had just come back from his trip, and I had no choice. I snuck one last look out into the sea, one final breath of the salty air, rejoiced in the song of the seagulls above, and that was it, I was back in the room.

I opened my eyes and glanced at the newly-sprouted

stubble on his beard. He smiled at me, and the air of a distant, foreign country filled the room. "Good evening," he said and embraced me gently like he was hugging a fragile China doll. I groaned bitterly at his soft touch. It always reminds me of how crippled I am. Fucking crippled.

"I heard the news. I see they want to add a specialist surgeon from New York to your next surgery. Don't worry, I heard everything. I'll make sure they go through with it. Don't worry, it'll be fine, we'll pay the surgeon whatever amount he wants. I'll personally make sure he comes to Israel," he stated with his usual confidence.

Unyielding optimism. That's just how he is. Always giving me the feeling that no matter how rough things are, we'll be able to weather it, as if he's the one controlling all the good that life has to offer.

"The last surgery failed... don't you worry about it, it's just a small setback on our way forward. Keep your head up high. I've already scheduled a talk tomorrow morning with the doctors and the specialist from New York. We'll set up everything, I'll convince him to come over and perform the surgery, and he might even show up next month, how does that sound?" He beamed with pride.

"Sounds great," I answered flatly and forced out a smile.

My dad always manages to convince me that hope is right around the corner, and that I'm crazy for not seeing it the same way. At times, when I take a close look at him, I can see how disappointed he is in me. He never said a word about my horrible crash, but I know that deep down, he's surely mad at himself, and mad at me for daring to do such a horrible thing.

My irresponsible act, my impulsive and thoughtless behavior, is radically different than my dad's calm and calculated attitude. My dad, who spends his days working at the lab, running clinical trials in an attempt to save humanity from cancer's grip, who partners with leading labs from all over the world, with experts in the field, who's always invited to speak at conferences to share his innovative insights—has a son who is the exact opposite, and is now crippled... unbelievable.

In truth, we couldn't be further apart. I, who can't sit still, a hyperactive kid who runs around all day looking to party with friends, and my dad, who hates exercising, hasn't played any sport since he was a kid, whose only physical activity includes moving the computer mouse, and whose daily dose of excitement comes from ardently inspecting minuscule cells with his microscope.

After all these years being my dad, it seems like he's still trying to get used to me (without much success). Honestly, you don't have to be a genius to know what he really thinks of me. I remember one time, when I came back from a party late at night, I saw him sitting by his computer engrossed in his work, and despite the late hour, and the stench of alcohol seeping from me, he said absolutely nothing. He just smiled at me, straightened his glasses, and went back to staring at the screen. One glance at his expression was enough to see how disappointed he was in me, how he viewed my behavior as childish. In his mind's eye, I'm like a kid who isn't willing to grow up, a kid who just wants to have fun all day and fool around.

Back in my hospital room, he stuffed a piece of chocolate into my mouth. My favorite Swiss chocolate he bought especially for me in Germany. I sucked on the small chocolate square and savored every moment. My dad spoke about the conference, the people he met, and the freezing weather in Berlin, but all I could think about was the lab, that dark night I hid under the desk and heard everything, changing my life indefinitely.

He placed another piece of chocolate in my mouth, but now, the sweetness of the cocoa grew bitter, to the point I felt nauseous. As he kept talking, I shut my eyes. I couldn't go on with this father-son act. He noticed my shift in mood.

"Are you okay?" he asked worriedly.

"Yeah, just a bit nauseous," I answered quietly.

"Do you want water?" he asked.

"No, thanks, I'm good." I contorted my face slightly. "Maybe I should sleep," I suggested.

"Now?" he looked out the window in confusion. "It's only seven in the evening."

"Yeah, I know, but I'm pretty tired," I lied, even though I hate doing this.

"Okay, I get it." He sighed. "I'll get going then. I'll go home, no worries. I'll be back tomorrow." He got up slowly and gave me a light pat on the shoulder. We exchanged smiles, and he left the room.

My nausea was growing worse. "If only I could sit up, that would great," I admitted out loud.

But I couldn't do it. Because this is how I am now, doomed to lie in this shitty position, on my back, forever.

"If only I could sit up now," I repeated out loud, my voice growing stronger with every word. "If only I could sit up now," I yelled and began to sweat.

"Ugghhh." I cried out even louder. "But you can't, can you.

You're fucking crippled, do you get it?!" I replied enraged, crying louder until I could feel the walls of the room tremble. My heart beat fast and my body was drenched in sweat.

"Crippled, you're crippled," I screamed as loud as I could.

I could've called the nurse and asked for anti-nausea medication, but at that moment, my ego controlled my emotions.

No. I didn't need help. I'd suffer instead. I'd suffer this nausea until it would pass on its own. I didn't need help from anyone. I felt terrible, frustrated, and sad.

It took me about an hour to stop yelling. My voice was raspy by then, and, late at night, exhausted from living, I shut my eyes and drifted off to a deep sleep.

3.

I open my eyes. Yeah, I wasn't wrong. I'm not alone in the room; it's clear to me. I can recognize her by the soft touch of her hand on my face. She's my love, my one and only, the best thing that has ever happened to me.

How dumb was I before the crash, to overlook this incredible thing? What were the odds of us meeting each other, falling in love, and dating? How did she even agree to go out with me? If I'm being honest, I didn't deserve her attention. As hard as it is to admit, I was so full of myself at the time. My "ego" controlled me to the point where I was downright awful.

Looking back, I feel ashamed. I treated her badly, just terribly. No matter how much I loved her, I always held myself back from fully giving in to my love for her, convincing myself that there was "more out there" to experience. Unbelievable, yeah, but that's what I used to say. If I would've kept those thoughts to myself, then maybe it wouldn't have been as bad, but I actually behaved that way—full of myself, arrogant, that's who I was, horrible. And she... just wanted to love, simply love. Unconditionally, with no ego involved. Just love. My sweetheart.

We met when we were seventeen, and what could one

truly expect from a seventeen-year-old couple, hormones raging and all? But after the crash, I realized that while we were only seventeen, it felt as if we had known each other our whole lives.

I felt the warmth of her hands on my face and imagined the comforting heat of her body seeping into mine, even though I couldn't actually feel anything from my neck downward.

I recalled an evening we shared on the roof, where we put up a kiddy's tent that was way too small for us. I remembered how we lay inside, our long legs spread outside the tent, and cracked up as we tried to stay still to avoid collapsing the tent. We didn't have any alcohol that night. We just laughed and laughed, in the most natural way.

"Who said we had to get inside a tent to see the stars?" I asked, and the two of us burst out laughing. We pressed our bodies together and gazed up at the stars.

I was so happy that night, it was probably the first time I'd left my ego at the door, far from the tent, and allowed myself to be authentic. It was just the two of us, crammed in the tent, feeling vulnerable, free, boundless. I felt drunk on love. We hugged, kissed, and giggled endlessly as if we were floating in a bubble that was just ours, disconnected from the rest of the world. The love I felt for her that night was unlike anything else. I remember stroking her hair away from her face, gazing at her eyes, and staring at her lips like it was my first time seeing her. "My Talila."

That night, I realized how much of an idiot I was. How much she'd fought for me, how much she desired to be with me, yet me with my arrogant attitude ignored her. Only then, on that night, in our little tent on the roof, everything became clear. Suddenly, my eyes opened to what she had seen months ago, and I finally let myself sink in and my heart roam freely. Agreeing to set my emotions free, I dove into that terrifying space, that space where my emotions control me, and not the other way around.

As I kissed her face, I mimicked different animal voices like they were nearing our tent.

"Oh no, don't you hurt, my Talila," I said playfully as I fought off the snakes, lions, and wolves. "Get out of our tent, evil animals!" Talila went along with it and pressed her body onto mine as if she was afraid, while I held on to her tightly and scared off all the menacing creatures. We were so... adorably dumb. We could've gone like that for hours. Neither of us lacked imagination, that's for sure.

That night, for the first time in my life, I realized that it was much easier to love, much easier to release the grip and let my emotions take the lead. The moment I unlocked the door to my feelings, I knew they were now in control. There was no way back. This experience was the exact opposite of what I was used to in competitive sports, where the name of the game is to overcome my emotions to win.

Okay, time to snap back to reality, from our warm little tent to the hospital. Sliding my eyes open, my soft gaze went up and down her body. "Perfection," is all I had to say. With her standing beside me, my disability felt like a double punishment. It's unbelievably hard to look at her, it hurts, it really hurts. At times, I want her to stop coming, to give up on me and let me go for good. But I don't think Talila intends on doing that. She's holding on to the wild idea that, at any moment, I'm going start walking again. That my body just needs one small tweaking, and everything will be fine. I don't want to burst her bubble, but the chances of me walking again are slim. There's no way around it, I'm a practical person, and if I'm being honest, I know that it's just a matter of time before she cracks, gets sick of me, and leaves. I won't be angry when that happens. It's understandable. After all, what does a girl like her need with a handicapped guy like me?!

4.

It's a holiday and the hospital wing is quiet with no visitors. It seems that everyone is at home with their families. It felt kind of lonely at first, but then I thought of Him, and I calmed down a bit, knowing He was here with me. Whenever He arrives, I feel a certain warmth travel from my chin to my forehead, all the up way to my scalp. That's how I know He is here, even before we begin to talk.

Conversation No. 1 Between Me and "My Bro"

- So, where exactly are you? Huh? I'm sure you get that question a lot, right?

- No. This might surprise you, but most people assume that I am above them, high up in the sky, so they don't bother asking.

- And is that true?

- No

- Then where are you?

- Right here

- Here, here?

- Whoever knows me, knows that I am not outside, but

rather, inside. So, there's no reason to search for me out there.

- Say, why do some people connect with you more than others?

- The connection always exists, and each one has their own way of doing so. Whether they want to contact me or not is their decision to make. I can't intervene.

- Simple as that?

- Precisely

- We barely talked before the crash, and that got me thinking... do people need to go through bad things to start talking with you?

- Not at all. Bad things, good things... these are all ways of classifying the events happening to you. Categorizing life this way makes it seem more organized. But your interaction with me depends solely on you, not on any external event. Each one has the opportunity to speak with me like a friend, a brother. I'm here, simple as that, and the choice whether to talk with me is yours and yours only.

- And what do you have to say to those who can't hear you, like me? Who talk, yet hear nothing from the other end. Those who try and reach out to you but no one seems to pick up.

- Keep trying, don't give up. I appear in many forms, and not all are explicitly clear, like conversations. I work in mysterious ways at times, ways that are known only to myself and the person I'm reaching out to. When that happens, they'll know that it's me. They'll understand that I'm responding to their call, that their cries weren't left unheard. I simply respond in my divine way.

5.

"Get up, you lazy bum." I opened my eyes, startled. My best friend, Tomer, dropped by for a visit. He was the only one who still acted like his true self around me, unlike my other idiot friends.

"Hey, what's up?" I smiled. "Wow..." I was really happy to see him.

"What's up, man?" he asked and pressed the button to adjust my mattress and lift it up. "You need a little higher, gramps?" He laughed, holding a large pizza box in his right hand. "Brought you some. I saw what they serve here for dinner... ugh." He pretended to spit on the floor. "And they call that food? Disgusting." He placed the box on my paralyzed legs.

"Is it hot?" I asked.

"You tell me," he joked and looked at my lower body.

"Come on, enough with your stupid tricks, I can't feel anything," I said and rocked my head from side to side.

"Nothing?" He raised a brow.

"Nothing, you idiot, nothing."

"We'll see about that," he replied and left the box just where it was on my legs.

Opening it, he took out a slice and drew it near my mouth.

I took a small bite. He sat down and grabbed a slice for himself. "Well, what do you say? Will I make a good nurse?" he asked and helped me grab another bite.

"You were born for this," I retorted sarcastically. "I missed you, man," I said while chewing rapidly.

"Wait, let me wipe your mouth, honey." His voice was high-pitch and trembling, like a gentle old nurse. "Wait, you have some here, and here too, sweetie." He wiped my face clean, and the two of us burst out laughing.

Man, I love this guy so much. It felt like ages since I laughed about pure nonsense. I missed that.

"You've lost it, bro, I'm telling you," I said.

"True, it's all true," he agreed as we kept on eating.

"Oh, wait." He suddenly remembered something. "Can you guess what your friend brought to drink? Water? Coca-Cola? Orange juice? Grape juice? Ta-da!" He took out two cans of beer from his bag and eagerly cracked them open. "I even brought my disabled friend a straw!" he exclaimed.

"You're really something, man." I let out a wide smile.

"'Why one need straw for beer?!'" Tomer mimicked the Russian vendor we both know well from the store back home. "'Straw is for woman! What, man take straw for beer?' He wanted to make fun of me for drinking this way, but when I told him it was for you... You should've seen his face! His smile wiped right off. I told him 'no, this is for my disabled friend, I think you know him.' 'Yes, I know your friend.' And then he muttered some curse in Russian. He was dying for me to get out of his shop."

"What an idiot, this friend," I mimicked his Russian accent and the two of us laughed.

"Huge idiot," Tomer agreed and placed the straw in my mouth and I chugged the beer as fast as I could.

"Wait, wait." He slipped the straw out of my mouth and moved the can away. "Are you planning on driving somewhere today?" We cracked up like two idiots. "Shh..." he said quietly. "I don't want anyone kicking us out of this fancy hospital. That's the last thing your parents need... to have you lying around the house all day like a statue."

I took a sip and nearly choked on the beer. "No, you're crazy." I coughed.

"Don't go choking on me like that!" He took out the straw and waited for me to clear my throat.

"Give it back," I said impatiently.

"Are you sure?" He made a worried face.

"I'm sure, yeah. Come on!" I was determined.

"Okay, okay, just no choking on the beer, yeah?" He slipped the straw back into my mouth.

"Much appreciated." I chuckled and began drinking quickly again.

"Between the two of us, I still think you're fooling us all," Tomer said and placed the empty can of beer on the bedside table. "Disabled and all, but you can finish a can of beer in less than a minute!" He punched me softly on the chest.

"Oww!" I yelled as if I was in pain.

"Oops." He pulled back.

"Just kidding man, come on, I can't feel anything," I said.

"You're such an asshole." He laughed and sipped on his beer, placing it next to mine. "So, what do you do here all day? Fantasize about Talila?" he asked as he sat near my bed and leaned forward. "Ahhh... Talila, my dear Talila." He mimicked her voice perfectly.

"You're a goner, dude." I cracked up.

"Can you feel me, can you?" Tomer asked sweetly, perfectly imitating Talia's voice, hugging me closer to him.

"You're a fucking idiot, man, for real," I replied jokingly.

"Tell me, what do you feel? What emotions do you feel?" Tomer went on.

"On top of the world, as usual," I replied cynically.

"Oh really, baby?" Tomer whispered in my ear seductively, struggling to keep his cool but ultimately giving in to the laughter. "Do you feel anything?" Tomer looked down at my body with concern.

"Nothing, nada, zero. How about you get off of me, man," I said impatiently but Tomer just pressed himself closer to me.

"But boo boo bear, I miss you." His voice was pleading and sweet.

"You're killing me, man! Your voice is perfect. I can't anymore, look at me, I'm crying with laughter," I said as Tomer wiped my tears. He brushed my hair back and looked me straight in the eyes like in some romantic Hollywood film.

"Boo boo bear," he said and tried his best to remain serious, but ultimately cracked up in my face. "Where did she come up with that name anyway, boo boo bear?" He lay on the bed beside me.

"I give good hugs, man, like a bear," I answered.

"Oh do you?" He shot an impressed face and handed us both a slice of pizza.

"Good thing the boys from the team don't know about 'boo boo bear,' he said while munching ravenously.

"True," I agreed.

"It's hard to be both captain and boo boo, don't you

think?" he asked and the two of us laughed again.

"There's more," I said as I took a bite of the cheesy slice.

"Really?" He smiled mischievously.

"I can't tell you though," I stated.

"Too bad. No more pizza then." He grabbed my slice just as I was about to take another bite.

"Oh you're evil." I frowned.

"Come on, out with it," he probed.

"You son of a... I'm going to be sorry for this, I know it." I rolled my eyes.

"Out with it!" Tomer pressed on.

"Okay, hand me the pizza and I'll tell you," I agreed. "You leave me no choice." Tomer let me have another bite. "Okay, okay, I'll tell you. Just because you're being annoying. There's more to boo boo bear, there's a whole family of names," I muttered under my breath.

"Who's in the family?" His eyes opened wide in fascination.

"There's cutie pie, sweet pea, and silly bear."

Tomer's hysterical laughter bounced off the walls of the dreary room.

"Ahh... I can't handle this anymore. My stomach hurts! Someone save me." He settled himself back on my bed and nearly choked on the pizza.

"Yeah, yeah..." I laughed along with him.

"This Talila... she killed us all, this girl of yours," he said as he finally calmed down and was able to chew normally.

"What about Talila?" I asked as I finished the last bite of pizza.

"Do you want more?" Tomer offered.

"No, thanks," I replied.

"What can I tell you, man." Tomer sounded serious. "She's quite the type, an unusual one." He sighed.

"So are you," I snapped as if protecting her.

"Yeah, but she's really something special, that girlfriend of yours." He lay back on my bed and slid his hands beneath his head. The two of us stared quietly at the ceiling.

"What?" I finally asked, a bit concerned.

"Nothing," he answered aloofly.

"Nothing?" I persisted.

"No, you know how she is... walking around school grieving, wearing all black, looking all depressed. I told her: 'Listen, lady, he's not dead, what's up with you?' She told me to shut up, so I answered: 'I'm telling you the truth, that's all.' Women, go figure. They're always so dramatic, aren't they?!" he asked but I didn't reply.'

The two of us lay in silence for a few minutes.

"And now?" Tomer turned his body around to face mine.

"Now what?" I asked, even though my mind was elsewhere. I was thinking of Talila walking around school, sad and confused, and it hurt terribly.

"You still don't feel anything? Nowhere? Are you sure?" he asked and turned to stare at the ceiling again.

"What are you talking about?" I asked confused and looked at his face.

"I'm asking if you feel something right now?," he repeated himself.

"Why...?" I was growing suspicious.

"Maybe because my hand is someplace special," Tomer declared mischievously.

"What?! You're crazy!" I yelled and spotted Tomer's fingers between my legs.

"You creep... there's a creep in here! Get him out!" I yelled and laughed.

"Well, I have to hand it to you man," he said. "That's it. I'm fully convinced you're crippled. Between the two of us, if you would've felt any sensation down there, you would've killed me on the spot, wouldn't you? That's it, you've officially passed my test. I officially announce you—a cripple. Wow, you're fucking crippled man, you truly are. I swear, up until this moment, I still didn't believe you." He stopped laughing and his voice grew solemn.

Tomer got out of bed, leaned down to his bag, and grabbed a cigarette and a lighter. He lit the cigarette and stood by my bed, scanning my whole body.

"I'm glad you're finally convinced," I said quietly.

"Yeah! I can't believe it. You're fucking disabled, man, I can't believe my friend is a cripple. I'll tell you what's the worst part? I've lost my beach partner. I mean, when it comes to dirt bikes, I know enough lunatics willing to ride with me, but where else will I find someone as crazy as you to catch waves with me every hour of every day? I'm telling you, man, you're one of a kind. Listen, you really fucked me up here. Note that down.," You could tell by his voice how disappointed he felt.

"Noted," I answered weakly.

A deafening silence filled the room. I really did fuck things up. There's no other way to look at it. Tomer moved away from my bed and stood by the window, smoking as he gazed out. I looked at his back. Whenever Tomer comes around, we talk about everything but the "elephant in the room." Neither of us are brave enough to confront it. Maybe this time, I'll be the first one to dive into it... I know I owe Tomer, above all people, an explanation for what happened that night. He was the only person who tried to stop me from doing the "anaconda" trick. As I thought of how to start, desperately searching for the right words, I heard footsteps nearing from across the hall.

"Someone is about to enter the room!" I cried out.

"How do you know?" He turned around.

"Trust me, I know everything around here. You don't have much time." I was nervous.

"Really?!" Without thinking twice, Tomer tossed the cigarette out the window, rushed to the bedside table and collected the beer cans, stuffing them in his school bag.

At that moment, Dr. Sweed opened the door, accompanied by a nurse.

"Hello," Tomer said amicably and faced them. "What a pleasant surprise!" He closed his bag nonchalantly.

"Hello, hello," the nurse replied cordially and Dr. Sweed didn't do much but tilt his head forward in recognition.

"Can I offer you a slice of pizza?" Tomer lifted the box above my legs and drew it closer to them.

"No thanks." The nurse smiled and Dr. Sweed remained indifferent and cold as usual. Ignoring Tomer, he picked up the medical file on my bed and began reading.

Tomer looked back and forth, first at them, then at me, then gave me a signal that he was leaving. "I think I'll head out, I don't want to bother you," he said as he arranged his stuff.

"Thank you," the nurse replied.

Tomer placed the pizza box on the cabinet. "Just so you know, this boy has passed my tests too. He really... uh, feels nothing, nothing. It's true, he's completely paralyzed," he stated.

The nurse and Dr. Sweed ignored him and continued to inspect my medical file.

"Well, I guess you guys don't listen much. Such kind people, indeed," he said and winked at me. "Anyhow, I need to go, I'm a busy guy, unlike my idiot friend here, this lazy bum." He smiled, leaned toward my bed, and whispered: "I'll head out, before something spills out of my bag if you know what I mean."

"Yeah, sure, go." I smiled back. "Tell people at home I say hi, don't forget," I added.

"I will." He picked up his bag and placed it firmly close to his stomach. "And you, young man," he said in a low voice, pretending to sound like an army sergeant, his favorite sort of voice to mimic when there are grown-ups around.

"Sir, yes, sir." I followed along.

"I advise you, young man, that by the next time I come around, you get your act together, do you hear me?"

"Of course, of course," I asserted like a disciplined soldier.

"Next time, I want to see better results, come on, try harder." He scrunched his brows.

"Sir, yes, sir!"

"I expect you to pull yourself together, stop with this childish act of yours, and return to us as fast as possible." Tomer kept the act going. He raised his voice and looked me dead in the eye. "We're sick of you being handicapped, do you hear me? Sick of it!" Tomer raised his hand in a fist. "Am I clear?" he asked and waited for a serious answer.

Dr. Sweed and the nurse exchanged startled glances, but Tomer didn't let that stop him and he hung on to his serious act until the last moment.

"Yes, sir!" I yelled back.

"Goodbye," Tomer said formally and walked out the door.

"Goodbye," the two of them replied, confused, trying to understand what just happened.

They looked back at me, but I kept my mouth shut. I wasn't going to tell them that my friend was a brilliant actor. I preferred to let them think whatever they wanted to. Honestly, I couldn't care less, and it actually felt quite good to see Dr. Sweed confused, forced out of his bubble into the real world around him. I didn't want to give them any explanation and kept quiet. Quiet and smiling. I pictured Tomer leaving the hospital, a satisfied grin on his face, proud of being able to confuse the grown-ups with his perfect sergeant persona. I know the guy, that's exactly what he was thinking when he left the place.

6.

The day of the surgery was drawing close, so close I could count the days. It's weird how things suddenly change when you feel hopeful, particularly the way you treat time. Instead of getting angry about all those wasted hours lying in bed, as I normally did, I decided to enjoy it. I began laughing with the medical team, listening to music, and having hour long talks on the phone with whoever was interested.

Of course, most of the talks involved me listening patiently as people shared details about their "cool lives" outside, but at least now, I was suffering a bit less than before. I tried picturing myself leaving the hospital and diving into the stories they told me, as if I was really there with them. I imagined myself getting caught on a field trip with some alcohol, being on a stage at graduation, standing in front of a crowd next to the host who forgot all his lines. I even pictured myself running along the steep hills during pre-boot camp training so I could get into elite units.

I listened to every single detail they said, just so I could form a clearer picture in my mind. I also picked up on how they were trying to downplay their experiences as if they were scared to make me jealous. It's okay, I can understand. I probably would've done the same if it was the other way around.

Conversation No. 2 Between Me and "My Bro"

- So, what do you say? Will the surgery succeed? Will I be able to walk again?

I finally released that nagging question that was haunting me for weeks since the surgery date was set.

- It's not in my hands.

- What do you mean it's not in your hands? Then whose hands is it in?!

- It has already been determined.

- What are you saying? That I can't choose whether to do the surgery or not?

- Not quite.

- Okay listen, I'm lost. What about my free will? Do I even have a say in this?

- Of course you do. You're free to choose your behavior, your thoughts, and your feelings. However, the surgery's fate has already been determined, a long time ago for that matter.

- A long time ago? Since when?

- Since before you arrived here.

- Here? You mean the hospital?

- No.

- Then where? Where exactly? I'm struggling to follow.

- Go further back.

- What? When? This year?

- Further.

- Further, where?

- Think.

- When? From the moment I was born? That far? It can't be.

- Why not? There's free will, but there's fate as well. Both exist in your life.

- So what are you trying to tell me? That there's a reason I ended up in my dad's lab? That sitting there under the desk and hearing what I heard was predestined to happen?

- Yes, moments like these exist in every person's life. They're inevitable, they happen anyhow, they're pre-destined.

- So what you're saying is, despite our free will, life is still full of unavoidable, fateful moments?

- Yes.

- So I can blame fate, and not me, for the fact that I'm lying here like a dead animal.

- It's not all about you, you know.

- What do you mean?

- When a fateful moment is determined, an inevitable one, it serves as a lesson for both you and all the people involved in the event. It wasn't destined solely for you.

- So what you're saying, if I understand correctly, is that the people around me, involved in my life, affected by this event... they too, couldn't have avoided it, it was their destiny as well?

- Yes. Your "crash," as you like to call it, is set on those people's timelines as an inevitable moment, a fateful one. There's no doubt that this crash has changed your life, but it's changed their lives as well. In fact, there's a large group of people who were affected by your crash, way more than you can imagine.

- Now, when you put it that way, I realize I've been so

focused on myself, that I forgot how many people have been suffering since my crash.

- Why suffering?

- What do you mean? Do you think they're enjoying watching me lie here like a sad piece of meat?

- Suffering is a choice. I never said they were suffering.

- What are you talking about? Don't you think it's horrible that my parents have to see me this way? That they have to nurse me like a baby? I'm sure you know as well as I do that my crash ruined their lives.

- Who's to say?

I could feel my insides burning. I bit my bottom lip, trying to find the right words without getting too angry.

- No? You think what happened to me isn't horrible? Do you think that I'm chilling here, having the time of my life?!

I felt like I could no longer contain myself, so I raised my voice even more.

- You think I'm lying in this fucking bed because I want to? Do you know where all my friends are right now? It's ten o'clock, and they... let me tell you, they're all at the beach right now, partying with beers in their hands, girls everywhere, sitting around a freaking bonfire! Do you get that?!

By this point, I was screaming in desperation.

- I'm here, and they're there, at the beach!

I bit my bottom lip furiously, so hard that a bit of blood dribbled on the white bedsheet, smearing it in dark red. "Shit." I looked at the dripping blood, but couldn't do anything to stop it.

A bitter silence spread across the room, and I was scared He might have left me here alone. I was quickly relieved when I heard Him speak again.

- This is just another event your soul has come to experience, that's all.

- Experience? What is there to experience, exactly? Pain, despair, suffering... is that what my soul has planned for me, to come to this world to suffer?

I was fuming.

- The soul knows no such thing as good or bad.

- And by that you mean?

- Forget the good and the bad. The soul has come to this world, after choosing this specific body to experience it through. That's all. The whole point here is the experience itself. Good, bad... those are definitions it knows nothing of. Only experience, development, and progress move it forward.

- So what you're saying is that I'm suffering now because my soul wants to experience this? It wants to experience being paralyzed? What a joy.

- I understand that you're angry, but this is how things work.

- Firstly, I'm not angry. Not at all! I'm freaking out, I'm fucking losing it! If only I could get up right now, I swear I'd tear this whole room down. I'm telling you, I'd do it! I swear.

I yelled frantically and looked down at the blood that kept on dripping.

- Anger is the most inferior reaction. The lowest one.

- So I'm not allowed to feel anger now, is that what you're telling me? Just a few minutes ago, I learned that I'm nothing more than a vessel for this so-called soul that has chosen me, a freaking masochist that wants to experience pain and suffering, and doing it at the expense of my life, and I'm not allowed to get angry? Perfect.

I grew quiet for a few moments, and when I saw He wasn't responding, I went on.

- And what about me in all of this? What about my feelings? My dreams?

- I don't think you fully understand.

- What?

I was impatient and furious, staring at the red blood stain that stretched menacingly across the white bed sheet.

- You, this is your soul. Your body, brain, thoughts, and emotions, are all in service of your soul. They come and go, just as swiftly as one changes a shirt, for precisely the right amount of time. But who always was, and always will be you, is your soul. Your eternal soul.

The conversation was cut off in an instant when the door opened, and the nurses that just swapped shifts entered the room to the sight of blood dripping from my lip. They instantly rushed to grab some wet wipes.

"What happened?" they asked frightened.

I couldn't answer, I was too busy contemplating the information I'd just received.

"I am my soul... but this can't be... why would I want to suffer so much, why would I want to lie in this bed for months, in this stupid hospital, paralyzed from the neck down? Why would I wish myself such immense suffering, what's the point in that?" I asked myself, but I had no answers.

The nurses left the room right after they treated my bleeding and changed my bed sheets. Even though I really wanted to continue my talk with Him, I knew it was over. I knew it was too late, we were done for the day, and there was nothing I could do about it.

7.

At night, a breeze gently blew in through a crack in the window, ruffling my hair. The strands tickled the skin of my face, but there wasn't much I could do about it. It soon began to rain, and a rejuvenating scent seeped into the room. Ahh… I inhaled... how much I missed the outdoors. I wanted to run as far off as I could. If only I could run with the wind and drench myself under the pouring rain, I wouldn't stop, not even for a split second.

Honestly, nights are the hardest for me. I can push through the days, but when night falls, it's a different story. I feel my weakest when it grows dark. I do whatever I can to stay awake, to avoid shutting my eyes and descending into the abyss. I keep myself awake for long hours, up until dawn at times. Only when I see the break of day do I let myself go and fall asleep.

Before the crash, I used to make fun of weak people who let fear take over their lives. They always seemed lame. I, on the contrary, wasn't willing to give in to my fears, and I'd always charge straight into them so as not to go under. If I so much as felt fear creep up, I'd tackle it mercilessly. Whether it was a massive, eight or ten foot wave, or the last few minutes as captain of a game whose final results were entirely up to me.

"This ain't nothing on you," I used to tell myself before charging forward.

I always knew that in order to win, I had to ignore the downward pull of my fears. Giving up wasn't an option.

Before the crash, I believed that the world split into two: weaklings who are controlled by fear, so much so that they are willing to give up their dreams, passions, and values to lead a plain, boring life. And the brave, who are willing to risk it all for their dreams. Unstoppable people who are eager to find out what the untraveled road has in store. The brave experience fear much like the weaklings, but they don't let it stop them. When fear comes up, they push through it. In some way, the weaklings envy the brave, even if they're not willing to show it. They know that the brave have chosen to live authentically—with all the risks, pain, and humiliation involved.

What always gets to me, is how the weaklings shamelessly make fun of the brave. They complain about them and hope that they fail, just so they could prove that it's better to play it safe. Fortunately, the brave stay true to themselves, and even if they fail, they get up and try again. The only thing they care about, above all, is winning. That was precisely how I felt before the crash, and now... now everything has changed.

Sunlight poured into the room, and I could finally take a deep, relaxing breath in. That's it, I could let go, the night has passed and I am no longer in danger. What had become of me, I wondered, now that I was just like those lame weaklings, like a little rat peeking out of its hole every now and then to grab some crumbs and rush back. What had become of me? How was I so afraid of the dark all of a sudden? Me?! Who wasn't afraid of anything in the past? This was madness.

8.

Outside my room, I could hear the familiar noise of bed castors rolling across the floor. Ooh... could it be? Were they bringing someone new to my room? There was room for another bed. I looked at the corner of the room, at the empty bed, the vacant bedside table, and the dormant monitor. It would actually be nice to have another person around, a bit of company. I wonder who they might bring in, someone famous? Someone young? Maybe a girl? Various "typecasts" raced through my mind, and I drifted far into the depths of my thoughts. Maybe they'd bring in a guy like me, an idiot whose life was ruined in a matter of seconds due to one stupid decision. I'd obviously spare him the pitiful glance because I know how much it sucks to be in his position. I won't put him through it. I won't give him a sorry look. I'll relate to him, like a brother. It sucks to be stared at like a caged fish in a sad aquarium, locked inside a glass rectangle, swimming hopelessly, with no option of getting out.

When it comes to me, everyone knows I wasn't run over, wounded in combat, or sick. Everyone knows the truth. Everyone knows that it's all on me, that I'm the only one responsible for the crash. I'm the one who took my perfectly healthy body to the edge. And that's why they pity me—they pity me not only for my dreary situation but for my stupidity as well.

The few seconds before I headed out riding are perfectly etched in my memory. I remember how I took my foot off the pedal and inhaled deeply, giving my friends a last look as they cried for me to stop from the opposing hill. I remember the moment I began to speed up, how I shifted my legs with all my might and headed out in a storm, as fast as I could.

Those moments flood my mind repeatedly. How exactly does this help? Why do I keep going back to this moment, time and time again? Why do I keep spiraling into this never-ending loop? I'm not sure. It's a total nightmare. And not only am I flooded with memories from that night, but I'm also continuously overwhelmed by a surge of the same feelings that caused me to do it in the first place. How did this happen to me? How did I, a person who was considered a master at controlling his feelings, let anger take over like that? How did I push myself into doing that anaconda trick?

I would've loved to forgive myself for making that decision, for that critical moment where I sped across with my bike. But I can't, I just can't. The truth is, I'm furious with myself. I simply can't believe it. How did I give in to my feelings like that and take it all out on a ridiculously extreme stunt? How did I put it all on the line so stupidly?

What would have happened, if I hadn't shown up that day, if I would've decided to go home after the game, instead of dropping by the lab? If only the weather was different, if only the field was empty that day, without any of my friends watching from the opposite hill, would I still have done it?

If only, and if only, and if only… I'm tired of this game. I'm sick of replaying it all in my head. I'm dying to let it go. Even though I'm the one to blame, I have to move on. Too bad there isn't some dumpster where you can drop by, leave behind all your baggage, and come out a new person with absolutely no recognition of your painful past.

Conversation No. 3 Between Me and "My Bro"

- I have to know, and I need you to give me an answer! I said that immediately when I felt Him in the room with me. That's how I am with Him, nothing too formal. We always pick up from where we last ended, so there's really no need to say hi, what's up, and such. I'm also afraid to waste my precious time with Him, as I'm scared He might leave me alone with all of my questions and never come back.

- Why did this happen to me?

I unleashed my rage.

- You surely don't expect me to answer that.

- Why not? I'd appreciate a hint, at the least.

- I think you have a few ideas in mind already.

- Sure I do. I've put together a few pieces of the puzzle, but everything is still a mess, and I really don't get how such a paralyzing thing (no pun intended), I laughed a bit before continuing, happened to such a hyperactive guy like me who is used to moving around all day. It's ungraspable.

- I can't help you with this, I can't do the work for you, there are no shortcuts. You need to figure things out for yourself. You need to ask the right questions and demand precise answers. There's only one thing I can tell you—now, that you've been lying in this bed for a while, you've finally managed to read the first word in your life's book.

- My life's book?

- Yes, the book that contains all the information about you. Information that you are supposed to figure out about yourself in this lifetime. This book contains all of the lessons you have come here to "fix."

- There's a book written about me?

- Every person has one.

- Can I see it?

- Of course not, you have to find things out for yourself. This is what you came here for. And not just you, but every other person in this world.

He kept silent for a few moments, then went on.

- You need to understand the reason you came to this Earth. What are the true reasons you were sent here for? You're just now reading the first word in your book, your long book of life, containing hundreds of pages and thousands of words.

- That doesn't sound despairing at all. I laughed nervously. Is my situation that bad? One word? Is that it?

- Most people in this world can't even read the first word, and they live their whole lives without ever reading it.

- Why?

- Because they don't care for it, they're busy.

- Doing what?

- Busy with external matters. They forget the internal and ignore the true reason they have come to this Earth.

- Well, what did you expect? We're pretty primitive down here. Most people care for things like work, money, kids, a house… and the little time they have left they dedicate to things like fun, that's it. Why would anyone have the time or patience to deal with those internal things you mentioned?

- But those things are important. You spend a lifetime unwrapping your gifts, without opening the presents themselves, without doing the real job you were sent here for in the first place.

Silence lingered in the room. He talked so fast that I needed time to digest everything he was saying.

- So, let me get this straight. That word you said, written in this big book of life…. I've taken a step forward by finding it?

- Yes, you definitely did.

- So what is that word I found?

- You tell me.

- Uhh…

I felt a bit nervous straining my mind to try and find a witty response.

- This isn't a test. Think for a moment. Since you've been lying here, what has changed the most?

- Apart from the fact that I'm bored as hell?

- Yes, apart from that.

- Well, I now see that before the crash I was… how can I put this… overly focused on myself, all day, every day, focused on nothing by my pleasure and my successes. And looking at things now from this bed, it all seems a bit… what's the word… egotistical.

- Exactly!

- Come to think of it, just between us, I feel ashamed for behaving that way. I look at the people around me who love me and I'm honestly surprised they even tolerate me.

- I feel your shame, I'm experiencing it with you, and I have to say, this isn't the first time this has happened to you. This isn't the first time you've felt how self-centered you were, it's just that this time you're also aware of it.

- What do you mean?

- I'm sure you know you were here before.

- I was?

- Yes, in this world. This isn't your first time here.

- Are you sure?

- Yes, why are you so surprised?

- Why am I so surprised? Well... where should I begin? Maybe because this is the first time I'm hearing this? I chuckled.

- If you really want to know...

He stopped for a moment.

- You've been through two hundred ninety-four incarnations. Yes, exactly two hundred ninety-four incarnations.

- What?

I was startled. My voice grew raspy as I slightly coughed and tried to pull myself together.

- Wait, what? What are you talking about? This isn't normal.

I swallowed nervously.

- Yes, it is your soul... he wanted to go on, but I put a stop to it.

- Wait! Enough! Hold on! Time out!

- What?

- What do you mean what? What are you talking about?

- Why are you so surprised? You've been here before.

- What do you mean by that? I just come and go?!

- Yes. You, and the majority of the world.

- You're saying all of this so nonchalantly as if I'm supposed to know this. As if this wasn't my first time hearing this. As if I've learned this in school or something.

- Don't you feel familiar with things in this world? Don't you ever get the sensation you've been here before?

- Well, when you put it that way, yes. But why so many times? Why would I come here two hundred ninety-four times? That is insane.

- I think so too.

- You do? I asked in surprise.

- Yes. I agree with you. Two hundred ninety-four reincarnations is a lot, but until you pass the lessons you came here to "fix" and move on with your book of life, it appears that you'll be coming here again and again.

- Really...? I still don't get it though, why come here two hundred ninety-four times, for God's sake?! Oops... I smiled bashfully.

- It's okay. Do you want to know why? I'll tell you why: because you spent your last incarnations focusing on things other, rather than the actual work you were meant to do.

- Wait, wait. So what you're telling me is that I'm here because I didn't do the work I should have, so this time, you've decided to go "all out" and punish me for it? Let me suffer as a handicap?

- Who do you mean by 'you?'

- You up there.

- Whoever chose this lesson for you was your soul, which, in simple terms, is actually you.

- I don't get it. I'm lost. You're saying I chose to be paralyzed?

- Yes.

-Why would I want this for myself? I'm suffering!

My voice grew loud and somber.

- I think this was the only way to reach some sort of result, so you can advance this time around.

- So what you're saying is that in order to advance in this book of life you mentioned, to read the words and do the job intended for me, I have to suffer?

- Not necessarily. You don't have to suffer. You can understand many words by experiencing the good, without any suffering. But for you, it didn't work that way. Another reincarnation, and another, and another, until there wasn't another option left but to take extreme measures to get you to wake up, wake up and stop messing around with superficial things, so you could focus on the real deal instead.

- This doesn't make sense.

My mouth was dry and bitter. I was furious.

- This isn't fair, this isn't fair.

Heat was building up in my body. I felt like screaming, kicking, and yelling, but I held myself from doing anything. I took a deep breath to calm myself down, then searched for the right words to keep going. We kept silent for a few moments, and then I went on.

- Don't you think this is all a bit brutal?

- It's more brutal to stay in place. To reincarnate continuously without so much as reading one page of your book, don't you think?

- No, I don't think so. You know what? I don't know, I really don't. I had it all before the crash, before that horrible night in the lab, and now I have nothing. And you're saying all of this is just for me to read one sorry word in a book? For me to realize how egotistical I am? Okay, then I'm fucking egotistical. I admit it. Come on. I'll work on myself, I'll get better. I'll volunteer, I'll do whatever it takes, I'll help blind people cross the street and visit kids sick with cancer. Come on, take it easy on me, help me walk again. Please…

My voice cracked.

- It's not that simple.

-Why? You're the boss, aren't you?

A tear trickled down my cheek and spilled onto the white bed sheet.

- I'll try to explain this so you'll understand better. I'll give an example from your world, okay?

- Yes, yes.

I tried holding back the tears, but they just rolled down my face uncontrollably, creating a soggy pool on my bed. I was overwhelmed by feelings of sadness, pain, and anger, but I didn't want the conversation to end. I needed to get a grip quickly so I could properly listen to what He had to say.

- Are you with me?

- Yes.

- Imagine there's a party on an island, a tropical party with music, delicious food, and great drinks. And you're there having fun. The party is nearly perfect, only there's one issue—all of the guests are children, they're all three years old, and you're the only grown-up there. The kids are cute and funny, and it's fun to hang around them, but after a while, you realize that this is all kind of… boring. Not suitable for your age.

- Okay, I get it.

- Now, let's say that on another island, far from your island, there's another party, just as great, where all of your friends are hanging out. They're all your age, and to get there, you need to dive into the deep end and swim in the dark until you find the right island. The way there may be dangerous, and you'll be going through several days of isolation, all by yourself in the great ocean.

- Okay, I get it.

- Would you go there? Would you embark on that venture?

- I'm not sure.

- That's exactly it!

- I'm not sure I understand.

- That's exactly your problem. You've been through two hundred ninety-four incarnations. You're stuck on the same island because you're not willing to jump in and find the right one for you.

- Why? Because I'm scared?

- No, you're simply used to it. You're used to living with three-year-olds, so it feels natural for you to waste your life on superficial, external phenomena. You're used to opening colorful wrapping paper but never the gift itself. Again and again, you choose not to jump in the water and not make the effort to look for the island that's right for you. You choose not to do your inner work, the most imperative vocation.

- So I'm stuck?

- You must now jump in the water and search for the island. You've spent too many incarnations on this island of children, like most people, who go about focusing on the external as opposed to the internal. Only now, after you hurt yourself, you decided to approach me, and make room for the right questions. I was always available for you, but it seems that you were always busy. I'm not mad, but that's how it was. You're obviously not too different from other people, who spend a lifetime without asking themselves existential questions like who they truly are, how did they get to this world, or whether God exists? For the most part, people are asleep. That's all. And they'll do anything, absolutely anything to avoid dealing with those questions, to stay on the island, never jumping in the water. True, they know that they will one day die, but it always seems so far away. They live thinking that they will go on living forever.

- I get it.

- You must jump, swim, and hold on tight so you can get to the right island. A surprise there waits for you.

- A surprise? I hope it's a good one.

- You'll have to find out for yourself.

- Yeah, yeah, I get it. No shortcuts.

- Don't be so sorry, enjoy the journey.

- I am, I am, look at how much fun I'm having.

I glanced at my paralyzed body, and a small grin appeared on my face. I couldn't see my bro, but I'm sure He was smiling too.

- Just so you know, I really enjoy talking with you.

- Thank you.

- No really, this isn't just about my crash, it's because... well, you know...

I was searching for the right word.

- Because?

- You know why.

- Me.

- Yes, you. I'm not talking to just anyone, I'm talking with you, the "big boss."

- Great, just don't go too far with it.

- What do you mean?

I asked, surprised by His answer.

- People treat me with far too much respect, to the point where they lose all interaction with me. I appear unapproachable. So I'd rather you see me as a close friend, one who has your best interest, who you can talk with about everything. Don't view me as this grand, holy, entity.

- But why, isn't all that true?

- Yes, it is. I'm perfect, complete. But if you want us to keep talking, you must treat me as an ordinary being, not a perfect one.

- Yes "boss."

9.

The day of the surgery arrived, and it seemed like everyone had decided to walk around with idiotic smiles on their faces. People were hopeful, and it felt like everything depended on this rare surgery to bring me back to life. The high hopes around me skyrocketed, breaking new records. I, however, decided to play it cool. I'd already been through my share of surgeries since the crash, so I'm more careful today when it comes to optimism. It works better for me that way.

As they led me into the operating room, the bright fluorescent lights of the hall blinded me. For a moment, I imagined myself as some actor from an action film, forcefully led into a torturous chamber. I playfully planned out an escape plan and looked for secret hatches in the ceiling, stairway, and elevators. I envisioned myself as I jumped off the bed and dashed to the exit. The only thing snapping me out of this action film was my mom and dad, who were accompanying me on both sides of the gurney. I've yet to see an action star holding his parents' hands... well, sure enough, they killed it for me. Okay, back to reality, I needed to get a grip and stop daydreaming so I could come back.

We stopped at the entry of the operating room, where

we hugged and said our goodbyes.

My dad made sure to remind me of how hopeful he was about the surgery. "This time, it has to work, you're coming out of this surgery and that's that, good as new! A bit of rehabilitation and you're back to walking," he stated confidently as if he was sending the message to my body so it knew just what was expected of it. I felt like one of his lab rats, who sacrifice their body for the sake of his clinical experiments. Maybe I was just like them, willing to roll with it and go through this dangerous surgery just to please him. If anyone would've asked my true thoughts on this, I would've replied that I'd rather stop with these surgeries and release myself from all of this. I would say that I want to be free, free from this ridiculously hopeful spirit, and with enough courage to acknowledge the hard, cold truth—I'm handicapped, fucking handicapped.

I smiled at my dad, or better put, forced out a smile. It was a friendly one, just like the one babies curl on their faces when they automatically mimic the person smiling at them. A smile without the knowledge of the person who is "doing" the smiling—was precisely how I felt.

Honestly, I had a horrible feeling about this surgery. It began in the morning when I woke up with a terrible sensation.

My mom crouched down and gave me a long hug. I could feel her heart beating fast. She didn't say a word, she just gazed at me silently, with loving eyes. I love how she can say so much without saying a word. If only I could. I'd tell her all about the crappy feeling I woke up with that day. I'd tell her my true thoughts, that I wanted to call off this surgery. But instead, all I could think about was the same question that had been flooding my mind since that night in the lab. Why? Why hadn't she told me? Everything could've been different if only I knew. If only she had told me the truth. I could've kept it between us.

I asked Talila not to walk me into the surgery, even though she desperately wanted to. I felt like it might be too much for me.

"Are you sure?" she asked with offended eyes when I broke the news to her.

"Yeah, it's at like six in the morning, super early. What were they thinking? Who operates at such an early hour? Oh, and also..." I said softly, and Talila leaned over to hear me better. "I've always wanted someone to cut open my back and mess around with my vertebrae, one by one when it's still dark out." I gave a menacing sneer.

Talila laughed. "You idiot." She hugged me tightly.

"No, really, now seriously. I don't get them. What? Were there no available hours left during the day? Why not choose an hour like nine in the morning when you're done with your morning coffee, or four in the afternoon after a good nap? Those are better hours. Don't you think?" I asked and waited for her answer.

"It's a long surgery, they have to start early. There's no other way, but don't worry, they know what they're doing," Talila reassured confidently, but I wasn't too convinced.

"Come on, would you rather do your math finals at six or eight in the morning?" I insisted on knowing.

"At eight, I guess." She shrugged.

"You see? That's exactly what I'm talking about. And this isn't a test, we're talking about slicing, cutting, and sewing... a full-on horror movie centered around my body, at six in the morning! Fucking six in the morning, I can't believe it."

We stayed quiet for a few moments until Talila broke the silence and said, "Wow... can you imagine what will happen if the surgery works? If you can walk again?" She was clearly trying to change the subject.

"And leave all of this beauty behind?" I asked and looked around the bleak hospital room, making both of us laugh.

"No, really, I'm serious," she said in a formal, principal-like tone. But I wasn't in the mood to fool around.

In general, I don't like messing with... what will happen if... instead, I preferred to hide with her under the sheets until we were out of air. I inhaled the sweet smell of perfume on her neck, and kissed her rapidly, then slowly, until I froze at a certain point with my lips pressing hard against her skin, and played dead. Talila, who always jumps in these moments, moved my face sideways frantically. I didn't move an inch, and gave her a cold, hard, lifeless look, until I couldn't handle it and bust out laughing. "Oh Talila, Talila..."

Her innocence always makes me laugh. Having her around is the only time I can truly forget that I'm handicapped. I let myself float off to a different world with her, a world in which I become the "old Yair" again, long before the crash.

It's the hardest when she leaves, and reality falls over me like a black curtain. Restless in mind and frozen in body, like a worthless piece of meat who can't do anything.

"So, what do you think? Will this surgery work?" she asked again, refusing to let go of the topic.

I ignored her and went on counting the freckles on her face.

"You're counting my freckles again?" She smiled.

"Shhh... don't confuse me, I'm counting. Last time I got to fifty-two freckles," I said in all seriousness.

She fixed her face in front of mine, like a model waiting for the photographer's orders, as I kept on counting every freckle and freckle. "Final number... fifty-three!" I announced like a sports reporter presenting the final results of a suspenseful game. "That's it, a new member has joined the team," I yelled happily.

"What will be the end of you?!" She laughed and traced my nose with her finger. "Can you be serious for a moment?"

"Sure," I replied and weirdly scrunched my face to make her laugh.

"Come on..." She sounded impatient.

"Come on..." I repeated after her, trying to pass the time. I knew where she wanted to take this conversation, but I couldn't do it. I knew, deep down, that she was still holding on to the idea that I would soon go back to my old self, and things between us would go back to normal. But in truth, I also knew that everything out there had changed. Everyone had moved on with their lives, and being stuck here meant that I didn't. That's the cold hard truth. Everything out there was moving, and I was here stuck in this bizarre time bubble, light years away from my previous life. The school year was about to end, and soon my friends would be drafted into the army, and then they'd move on with their lives, and I... what would become of me? Even if I ever left this place one day, what exactly would I be returning to? Everything I previously had, was no more. The train left the station and moved on without me. That's it. I get it. That's how things are now.

The medical assistant led me into the operating room,

and as the doors behind me closed, I gave my parents one final glance. The smell of antiseptic, as well as hazy lighting and a piercing chill welcomed me into the room. I became cold in an instant and could feel goosebumps all over my body. I remember laughing with the nurses and joking about how their real plan was to freeze me for the next ten hours, and instead of operating, would throw a wild party in the room without anyone knowing.

"Am I right or am I right?!" I asked Dina and Judith, the two chubby nurses who laughed hysterically at my question. Maybe because the wildest thing they'd done in the last century was to inject morphine into agitated patients. Still, that didn't prevent me from diving into my imaginative world where these two chubby nurses were having the time of their lives in a party I threw in my head.

I didn't ask for a blanket or to change the temperature. I didn't say a word. I just wanted them to start and get it over with. I'd been waiting for this surgery for three months and I was extremely ready for it.

Into the operating room entered an American doctor who flew in especially for me from the U.S. He heard I was a surfer, so he showed me some cool pictures of him surfing in Maui. A few minutes into our conversation and the two of us had drifted off into some bubble of our own. Like two surfer bros, we talked about surfboards, insane waves, and the best beaches to surf in the world as if these were the most important things on earth. Honestly, we could've kept going for hours, but Dr. Sweed entered the room at one point with his serious face and killed our vibe.

The American put his phone back in his pocket and gave

the anesthetist the okay to begin. I closed my eyes and took a deep breath. The anesthetist placed a mask on my face and I began to count backward until the anesthesia began to spread all over my body. I remember those few moments of dozing back and forth between states of wake and sleep. And I remember the moment before I completely blacked out, the moment I returned to my dad's lab and to everything that happened there.

"What are you doing here?" I asked myself. I was hiding under my dad's desk. I didn't plan for things to turn out this way. In fact, I wasn't even supposed to be there. We just won the local soccer game, and dad, who is a big fan of winning, simply had to hear the news from me. He never found the time to go to my games because he was always so busy, and it also didn't really interest him, so I decided to stop by his lab and surprise him. I loved hearing him roar his victory cry with pride. It's kind of scary for those who hear it for the first time, but I'm already used to it. Sometimes, he would take things one step further, go all the way, and pick me up on his back, as if I was a wounded soldier, and run around in circles.

Even though it was late, I decided to go to his lab. We'll probably grab a bite later on, I assumed. I remember thinking hard about what I felt like eating and running through all the nearby restaurants we could go to.

I walked past the guard at the entrance of the building and smiled at him. I could've rushed past him like everyone else and gone straight up to the lab, but, as part of my commitment to "look out" for those we usually overlook, I decided to stop and talk with him for a while.

A few years ago, I decided to notice the people we don't really pay attention to. The people working odd jobs, who are seen, but not really acknowledged: security guards, drivers, cashiers, and such. It always felt a bit sad that no one ever noticed them. Like it wasn't enough that they were being overworked and paid a shit salary, they also had to deal with the feeling of being invisible to the rest of the world. And to think that they woke up each morning to work with that sucky feeling that no one really cares for them, that all society needs from them is to play a certain role, that's it. It must be horrible to live that way, to suffer that daily humiliation. At least I think it is. So I decided I'd do the exact opposite—I'd pay attention to those "invisible" people, and every time I ran into one, I'd stop and talk with him, dedicating a few minutes of my time.

"So, what's up, guard?" I asked as I gave him my bag.

"Fine," he replied flatly.

"I'm just coming back from a basketball game... man, we had a great run today. And you wouldn't believe it, I broke a record by slam dunking three times in a row!" I exclaimed proudly.

"Basketball?" he asked.

"Yeah, yeah, basketball. What about you, do you play anything?" I tried to throw the ball back at him.

"Sometimes." He smiled a bit and flashed his gold front teeth. "When I find the time, I play soccer with my kids."

"Where?" I asked, even though he'd already finished checking my bag.

"At the park near my house, on Saturdays," he said as he scanned me from top to bottom.

"How many kids do you have?" I asked.

"Two." He seemed surprised that I was interested.

"Are they little?"

"No, big fellas. Fifteen and seventeen," he said and signaled with his hand above his head so I'd see they were taller than him.

"Fellas?" I smiled and he smiled right back.

"Are you here to see your dad?" he asked after a moment.

"What, you've seen me before? You know my dad?" I asked surprised.

"Yeah, I've seen you around here a few times, walking out of the lab with your dad," he explained.

"Oh, I didn't know that," I stated.

"Yeah, your dad is a hard worker, truly. He arrives early in the morning and leaves late at night, every day," he said.

"Yeah, the guy's on a mission, he wants to save the world. That's just how he is," I replied proudly.

"Save the world from what?" he asked curiously.

"Cancer," my voice grew serious.

"I saw him on TV, he's an important guy. I was important once too, in Russia. I was a chemist," he said, and I could hear a bit of sadness in his voice.

"You studied chemistry?"

"Yeah, I have a master's in chemistry," he replied.

"Nice!" I said.

"Nice, huh... well, how exactly does that help me? In Israel, I'm nothing but a security guard," he declared.

"At least you're watching over labs." I laughed.

"True, that's something," he said and let out a small laugh.

As more people gathered at the entrance, I moved forward and said goodbye.

"Well, my brother, the security guard, I'm going in. I'll talk to you later!" I said and walked toward the elevators.

"Sure!" He smiled and began looking through the purses

of the people behind me.

After a few minutes of conversation, I could already see the shift in his mood. From a numb guy who barely said a word, to someone who smiled and laughed, all because of a word or two that we exchanged.

Knowing that my dad was such a big shot always made me a bit nervous. I'm proud of him, of course, but it's more complicated than that. After all, I'm his only son, and I can sense that he expects certain things from me, even if he doesn't say them to my face. I don't need words to know he has huge hopes for me. This issue has always made me nervous. What about my dreams? What about what I want? What is my place in this world, and what will I do with my life? This issue was always on my mind. The footprints my dad etched into the world are so grand, that at times, I feel there's no more room left for mine.

My dad and I are worlds apart. It's truly insane... I wake up each morning to surf, ride my dirt bike, play basketball, win, and feel most alive when there's adrenaline pumping through my veins. You can even say I'm addicted to that high. And my dad? The guy's on the other side of the spectrum. He's not able to get me. My love of sports has always seemed a bit childish to him, like I was stuck in some playground where kids are too busy playing games instead of stepping out into the real world of grown-ups. As if I'm stuck there with no way out.

My dad, who, when he was a kid, already had plans to save the world, and me, who... who even am I? I'm just looking to move, to challenge myself in different ways. Dad is calculated and meticulous, and I'm hyperactive, wild, and restless. From morning to night, he's busy with his projects at work, growing his research team, fundraising from all over the world, and participating in TV shows willing to host him. Everything so that the world could hear about his revolutionary ideas to save the world from cancer. And I... I'm only busy with finding the next new activity: like skydiving, ice hockey, or diving with sharks, and adding them to my list of activities that I carry everywhere.

Honestly, I have no idea where he gets his energy from. He wakes up before us and goes to bed after us. At times, I catch him in the middle of the night working, with the TV on in the living room. Working while listening to the news. Now and then, he takes some time off to hang out with mom and me in the evening. We know it's just a matter of time before he gets back to work, so we never get too excited. After all, we're just the backdrop of his life's story. We're just the background of his journey on his way to fulfilling his dreams.

He doesn't know this, but I call him "Mr. Perfect." Once, when I was little, there was a funny TV show for kids, and each character was named after a main trait that characterized them. I thought to myself that if my dad would've played in it, he would surely be named "Mr. Perfect." Yup. That name suits him. It made me laugh at the time. I remember lying on my living room floor and giggling to myself about the name I made up for him.

True, he might not stop to talk with the security guard in his building, even though he must have passed him hundreds of times. And true, he'll never come to see me play basketball with the rest of the dads, and he also can't bear to hear my mom complain for more than two minutes. But still, for me, he'll always be "Mr. Perfect."

My dad has suffered more than his fair share of criticism over his work, coming from people in the field who described his project as a "total failure." Those who state that my dad's project isn't financially reasonable and that the only reason he's able to raise millions of dollars and draw hundreds of people in is that he's good with words. In their opinion, it's just a matter of time before my dad's project fails immeasurably. Dad normally doesn't acknowledge them much and moves forward confidently. There's only one goal in mind for him, and that's to beat cancer and free this world from this deadly trouble that kills hundreds of thousands of people each year. Dad is sure he'll reach his goal, despite the setbacks along the way. Did I or did I not say he was Mr. Perfect!?

When I walked into the lab from the big hall, the door, which one normally needed to ring the bell for it to open, was open this time, so I entered without a problem, and I recognized him sitting at the corner of the hall with his back facing me. He was alone, so I decided to surprise him. I crouched on the cold floor and began crawling slowly and quietly, sneaking under desks along the way so he wouldn't see me.

I imagined I was some soldier on the lookout for the enemy, and had to do everything as carefully as possible because my life depended on it. I advanced to his desk, stopping to look at the space between the desks to see if he had caught onto me. The plan was to get real close to him and then hop up and surprise him. This was going to be just another one of my crazy surprises. Dad loves these kinds of things, and he also enjoys startling me whenever he can. It's this silly game we've been playing for years.

It took me about ten minutes to crawl to his desk. My head was a few inches above his shoes, as I breathed in and out slowly, proud of myself for succeeding. I decided to wait for the right time before putting my plan into action. I inhaled quietly and peered at his nonmatching socks. They made me laugh. And then, a moment before I was about to jump and reveal myself—it happened, I realized he wasn't alone.

By his desk, sat another woman. He wasn't alone as I initially thought. What I heard under the desk afterward made me freeze in place. What happened that evening, wasn't supposed to happen. Why did it have to happen with me there listening? Why did this happen to me? Out of all people? I honestly don't know. Maybe this was all meant to be, maybe this wasn't pure chance, maybe it was my fate to wind up there, just like my bro had said.

When I think about it, I can't give it any other name but fate. It seems like the whole event was planned out. How did I turn out to be in exactly the wrong place at the wrong time? If I wouldn't have been there, if I hadn't gone to the lab, then I would've gone straight home from the game like I first planned, and everything would have ended up differently. I can now see how inevitable this all was.

I lay there under Dad's desk, breathing quietly, completely still, trying to hear the words they said.

They worked in silence, each at their own desk, and I waited patiently for them to say something. I peered from under the desk with caution and looked at the woman. Her eyes were pressed closely to the microscope, and she was typing rapidly on her keyboard. I could recognize who she was. She was the young woman Dad had told me about, that same one who had just finished her chemistry studies at the university and who he fought over for weeks to recruit to his research team. She wasn't just young, smart, and driven, she was much more. Dad described her as a "super B.W.B." Meaning: "brain without boundaries."

Everyone on his team was, of course, a B.W.B. All of them, from research assistants to doctorates with years of research experience, who had come from top universities around the world. But this lady, this "super B.W.B.," had no professional experience whatsoever. She was the youngest on the team, but Dad knew what he was doing, and told all of us that this "super B.W.B" was something extraordinary.

After a few moments of silence, they began talking, and yes, it was just like I'd thought. They brought up chemical compounds, acidity indices, and the clinical trial that was bound to start the following day. I was inclined to crawl back out and enter the lab like a normal human being, but I didn't want to get up. Just the thought of them seeing me spy on them from under the desk was enough to make me die of embarrassment. So I preferred to stay in place and lie still. I listened to them talk about technical issues related to the upcoming experiment and made peace with the fact that I was doomed to stay there until they left the lab. They kept on talking, and I dozed off with thoughts about the incredible game, repeating those insane moves I had made on the court back and forth in my mind. Maybe I sucked at spying, but I was a pretty good basketball player… I thought and laughed to myself.

Finally, after about an hour, Ms. "Super B.W.B." got up and said she was calling it a night.

"It's getting late," she said as she packed her bag.

Dad got up too, and I assume he stood quite close to her because I couldn't really see anything at that point.

Her phone rang and she spoke softly. She said "yes" twice and ended the call.

"What happened?" Dad sounded worried. "You look pale."

"I have to go," she answered with a trembling voice as her footsteps neared the door.

"Wait a second, what happened?" Dad walked after her.

"It's personal, I don't want to bother you with it." She sighed.

"Nonsense. Talk to me, what happened?" he insisted and Ms. "Super B.W.B." sat back down.

Dad took a seat next to her.

A few moments of silence passed and I shifted carefully to the nearby desk and lifted my head so I could hear them better. I was curious. Surely a broken heart or some fight with friends, I thought.

"The results came in. It's what I feared the most. I can't believe this," she said and began crying softly.

Dad went to get her a glass of water and rushed back to her seat. A deafening silence lingered in the lab, and all one could hear was the ticking of the large clock on the wall. I breathed quietly and stayed put. Don't blow your cover now, I told myself as I hung onto the desk and leaned on it so as not to move.

"What results?" Dad asked.

"The lab results. Eviatar just called to tell me the news. It's what we were most scared of," she repeated and bawled uncontrollably.

"What?" Dad asked softly.

"Just like we thought... Eviatar... he's infertile. I can't believe it! Infertile!" she repeated the word, nearly screaming by that point. Dad got up and probably went to get her some Kleenex because when he came back, I could hear her blowing her nose.

"I get it," Dad said.

"Now, after so much time trying to get pregnant, we decided to finally see what the problem was, and what we were most scared of has actually happened. I can't believe it. It's horrible, it's not fair," she uttered loudly.

"It's tough," Dad agreed.

"Of course, in the beginning, we thought I was the problem, but it turns out, that everything is fine with me. It's horrible," she declared angrily.

"What a thing..." Dad uttered under his breath and the two of them sat still for a few minutes.

"It's funny that this happened just now... you telling me something so personal with just the two of us in the lab," he stated.

"Why?" she asked and blew her nose.

I wondered why as well, my mind brimming with curiosity.

"I don't believe in chance. What's happening now is interesting," he said.

"What are you talking about?" she asked and blew her nose again.

"Listen to me, I can see you're extremely upset, and that you're struggling to accept the news, but I want you to listen... I have something to say about it. This isn't the end of the world."

"What?" What are you talking about? I don't get it," she asked impatiently, and I remember asking myself that as well. *What is he talking about?* I wrapped my fingers tightly around the foot of the desk so I wouldn't fall, and held my breath in anticipation.

"This isn't easy for me," he said and I could sense the hesitation in his voice. "But I'll share this with you, just because this is such an ungraspable coincidence. As I said before, I don't believe in pure chance. I never told this to anyone. But I can let you in on something personal that can help you, that can give you power."

"Why? What do you mean?" she asked.

Dad didn't respond right away, rather, he waited a while before moving on.

I waited, tense and curious, my body aching from hovering in mid-air in this unnatural position. I didn't care, though, the only thing that interested me was hearing what he had to say.

"Listen," Dad finally said. "I'm going to share this with you, even though I never told anyone before. I'm doing this for you, just so you know that at times, we don't have control over what happens, but things can still turn out for the better, it's not as bad as you think."

"I'm listening," she said softly.

Dad took a few moments to himself and then finally said, "I'm also infertile." His voice was sullen.

"What?" she sounded surprised, and every hair on my body stood up.

"Yeah," he replied hoarsely. "We also found out when we tried to get pregnant and nothing worked. The tests were proof of it. I'm infertile."

"And Yair?" she asked immediately as if reading my thoughts.

"Not mine. We decided to keep it a secret, and a secret

we promised never to speak of," he stated firmly.

"And Yair... does he know?" she asked.

"No, and he'll never know. Only Danit and I know this secret, there's no need for bringing Yair into this," he insisted.

A piercing sensation cut through my stomach. I could barely breathe, and I leaned myself completely on the desk's leg so I wouldn't fall.

"What are you saying... that no one knows about it?" she asked.

"No one, just Danit and I. And no one needs to know about it. So I suggest you do the same. Keep it between you. It will be your secret, just between you two. From the moment Yair came into this world, he knows just one thing and one thing only: that I'm his father, and that's all he needs to know." Dad spoke with such assurance, and I remember that that was the moment I began boiling with fury.

Apart from the massive shock of hearing the news, I was angry at how confident he was, and how reassuringly he talked about the whole thing. As if he dictated the situation, and that was that, like I had no rights of my own.

I remember thinking, Why? Why did he decide I didn't deserve to know?

"Just so you know, there are thousands of kids being raised by non-biological parents, and most of them don't know about it," Dad said, sounding very convincing.

"Wow, he's seventeen, isn't he?! And he doesn't know to this day?" she asked.

"No. He'll never know. That was the ultimatum I gave Danit. She wanted us to tell him, but I disagreed. I told her from the get-go that the only way I'd be willing to go for a sperm donor was if Yair wouldn't know about it. Would it do any good if he knew? It would just make him sad, it's completely unnecessary."

"I see... thanks for sharing this. I appreciate it," she whispered under her breath.

"I feel like this moment was guided from above, this didn't happen by chance," he said.

"Yeah, this is insane. Unbelievable, what are the odds that such a rare thing would happen to the both of us?!" she said and got up from her chair.

"Okay, I need to think this through. I... I'll talk to him... of course, I won't tell him your story. Your secret is safe with me," she said.

"Thanks," Dad replied.

Her phone rang and she quickly answered it. A few seconds later, she said, "Okay, I'm leaving," and ended the call.

She picked up her bag and walked toward the door. "Thanks," she said as she stood at the entrance.

"You're welcome, good luck with everything," Dad said. She turned around and slammed the door forcefully, causing the whole lab to shake.

I lay on my back beneath the desk, frozen, trying to process everything I heard. I could've yelled, exposed myself. I could've jumped up and confronted him, but I didn't do any of that. All I did was lie on the floor without moving, reciting the words I'd just heard: "He'll never know anything." Why? Why didn't I deserve to know? After all, this was my life! Feelings of anger and sadness overwhelmed my body, flooding every part of my being. I tried to make sense of things, to get a grip, to control the surge of emotions taking over, but I couldn't. How could he have been so calculated, so cold? This was my life we were dealing with, the truth about my life! I've been living a lie for seventeen years, and he couldn't care less...if this was up to my mom, she would've told me a long time ago. I know her, the only reason she didn't say anything was because of him. Because she promised him. It's obvious. The more I thought about it, the angrier I felt. It washed over me like a menacing wave, sucking me downward, all the way to the dreadful bottom.

About an hour later, the light turned off and Dad left the lab, closing the door with a bang just like Ms. B.W.B. I stayed there, lying in the dark. I remember feeling cold and hungry, but not caring much. I just stayed there, glued to the floor, struggling to process what I heard. I was shocked. I felt horrible, as if someone had chainsawed my heart into two.

I remember leaving the lab and speeding away with my bike toward the field. Detached from my surroundings, I crossed a red streetlight. I was furious. How in the world did he dare... how could he... the thoughts ached the more I thought about them.

When I got to the field, I planned on being the only one there. But nearly all of my friends were present, and I had to take out my energy somehow. Going from that point to pulling off the anaconda trick wasn't too hard. It was, obviously, totally senseless, and a few of my friends really tried to stop me, particularly Tomer, but it was futile. I wanted to do it, and that was the end of it. I was that determined.

I guess I was so mad that all of my common sense just disappeared.

I always loved pushing myself to the limit, but pulling off the anaconda trick was more than simply "pushing." It was more like "destroying" my limits. On that dark night, I decided to forget about the bottomless gap between the hills, I decided to ignore the slim chance of pulling off the trick and coming out alive. The only things controlling my brain at that moment were feelings of anger, frustration, and terrible pain. I guess I left my common sense back in the lab under the desk.

I was angry at my dad, angry about everything. I remember taking a few deep breaths before hitting the pedal. Maybe that was the sane side of me that tried talking some sense into the mess I was in. I looked at my friends who sat on their bikes on the opposing hill, and I could hear Tomer yell, "Yair, stop! You're insane! Yair no!"

They all had terrified looks on their faces, as if they were staring at a demon. But I couldn't care less, and decided to go for it anyway.

I remember asking myself, "Why are they looking at me like I'm insane? Like I lost it?" But instead of dwelling on it, I brushed it off and ignored them.

If I'm being honest, a second before I went off, I knew it would end badly. I had a very bad feeling about it all, but despite that, I felt like I had to do it. Maybe, deep down, I believed that by pulling this off, I'd also be erasing everything I heard back at the lab.

It was the moment of truth, and I hit the pedal to kick off the anaconda trick. I sped across violently, riding as fast as ever to reach the edge of the hill at full speed. I knew that the faster I'd ride, the chances of me making it in one piece to the other side were higher. I raced to the edge of the hill, and at that point, I could've still given up the move, all I needed to do was jump off the bike, even if that meant turning and falling on the ground. I'd probably get some bruises and all, but nothing too serious. I was used to it, it was no big deal, yet I still decided to continue.

I rode, faster than ever before, to the edge of the cliff, and then it happened—I left the solid ground below and floated mid-air, hovering for several long seconds, a menacing abyss peering at me from below my feet. I remember looking at the opposite hill, and knowing, at that moment, that I was a goner. I was too far, and had absolutely no chance of getting there. I knew that I was about to spiral down the gap and crash, and there was nothing anyone could do to help. I was lost.

10.

A few hours later, the surgery was over.

It was time for me to get up, but I couldn't do it. I heard them call my name and light a flashlight over my pupils in an attempt to find some sign of life, but I was so far away by that point, elsewhere.

I heard them trying to wake me up, calling out my name, even whispering, but I couldn't answer. I suddenly realized that something horrible had happened. True, my eyes were open, and I could see them, but I couldn't react. Maybe this was temporary, or maybe for good, I couldn't really tell in those moments.

An hour later, though, I began to grasp what was happening. It became clearer by the minute, there was no escaping from it. The only thing I had left, my face, was now paralyzed as well. What a disaster.

I was drifting between two worlds, between here and there, worn out. I wanted to speak but I couldn't. "How is this possible?!" I thought to myself exasperatedly. "What if this is actually happening? What if I lost the only thing I had left in this world? If so, this is mad. My face... my face... the one thing I still had control over, the only thing I had left here. What if I... lost it too? This is horrible."

I always knew that my face was the only thing keeping me alive here during these long months in the hospital. It was the only reason. It was only because I could talk and feel people's touch on my face, that I had the will to power through things. "And now what? Now what?! What if I'm completely paralyzed? What will I do now? What if I lost it all? That's it, is there nothing left?"

Voices I hadn't heard before began calling me after them. It felt like they were inside my head, pleading with me to follow. I was dragged after their tug, into dark places, foreign and silent. I felt like I was slowly spiraling, descending further and further into their grip, losing all control.

At first, I followed their instructions and drifted off with the voices, but the further I went, the farther I got from the hospital, from the people surrounding my bed. Their voices grew weaker, and suddenly, it hit me. I froze out of fear. I knew that if I were to follow the voices, I'd part from this world. If I allowed myself to get dragged after them, I would officially be gone.

"What am I doing?" I anxiously asked myself. "What if I follow these voices, and never find my way back?" The uncertainty was frightening.

"Stop!" I yelled to myself. I felt that if I were to take one more step after these voices, that's it, there would be no coming back. I'd be leaving this world for good. The fear was real, I knew this wasn't just my imagination. This was the truth.

The voices kept calling after me, again and again. They were committed to the task they came here to complete, and despite my refusal, they pressured me to move forward.

I blocked my ears to drown them out. It was clear that if I wanted to stay here, I had to fight.

"I'm not leaving, get out of here!" I screamed at them.

"What happened to me?" I tried putting together the pieces to get a clearer picture. The only thing I knew for sure was that the surgery had ended, but instead of waking up in the rehabilitation room, I was stuck here, drifting in this blurry space between two worlds. I had no answers, just questions.

"I have to save myself," I repeated again and again. "This isn't my time to die, I'm not ready to leave yet." I was determined. If I were to leave now, there would be no coming back. Everything I knew, everything I know, would just vanish.

"I have to fight, I can't give up, I'm not done here yet, I'm not ready to leave."

People walked in and out of the room all day long, and when night fell, I was left alone. Honestly, I was scared. Being in the dark was rough.

"It's fine, everything is fine, I just need to survive the night." I tried calming myself down as I breathed heavily. I even hummed some children's lullabies to ease the nerves.

"I'll survive this night, I know I will." I was barely breathing and my body was drenched in sweat, but I kept my hopes up anyway. I was scared to shut my eyes and fall asleep. If I did, that would mean losing to the voices.

"I must stay awake," I told myself again and again, staring at the bit of light coming from outside. "Just don't shut your eyes, don't fall asleep. I have to stay awake, minute after minute, hour after hour, I must."

Time went by slowly, despairingly slow. I would've liked

to know what time it was, and how many hours were left until the morning, but there was no clock in the room, and the more time went by, the more I lost track of it. I felt like I was warping into an utterly disorienting darkness. I tried counting the minutes, the seconds, but my counting just smeared and faded, causing me to drift off to the place I feared the most, to sleepiness, darkness, to the voices awaiting me.

"Wake up!" I yelled, and the shock of the cry snapped me back in the room. Time went on, and nothing happened. I looked out the window repeatedly to see if there was a shift in the color of the sky, but there was nothing but pitch black. It felt like the longest night of my life. I just couldn't see the end of it, it went on and on until time no was no longer a concept I could genuinely grasp.

"How long has it been since the surgery? How many hours until sunrise?" I asked myself, confused as ever. Every now and then, my eyes shut, but after a few seconds, I'd open them and return to the room. "I must stay awake!" I exclaimed repeatedly.

Fighting off the voices wasn't easy. They weren't using any physical pressure against me, they were just calling my name obsessively, asking me to join them.

There were moments when I saw the voices as little transparent figures signaling me from afar. "Come on, move along. It's time to go." They pressed as if I had no other choice.

If it was up to me, I would've preferred things to get physical. At least that way, we could've battled it out and the best man would've won. But the voices came from a place where things didn't work that way. The rules of their game were completely different, it was more like a battle between brains, an absurd battle between my needs and theirs. It felt like they were everywhere, surrounding me from all corners, blocking any chance of escape. Even shutting my ears didn't help much, they were everywhere, inside and out.

I tried answering and screaming, "Go away! Leave me alone!" But that didn't help at all. They just ignored me. It felt like there was no one listening on the other side, as if they honestly didn't care about me. As if they had a mission on hand that they had to execute, whether I wanted to play along or not, and that was all there was to it.

Only when I saw the first light of day, I began to ease a bit. "Oh." I sighed. "Finally, this long night is over. That's it, this nightmare is over. Maybe things will be easier now," I cheered myself up.

I scanned the room; it wasn't the same one I'd been in before the surgery. I tried picking up on noises or voices of the staff outside the room, maybe I'd recognize one of them, or maybe I'd hear the murmurs of visitors waiting out in the hall. However, I couldn't hear a thing, not even the wheels of creaking beds being pushed down the hall. All I heard was silence. Pure silence. A deafening one.

"This is probably the quietest department in the whole hospital," I told myself as I looked around the room, trying to figure out which department I was in. I looked for the large letters usually printed on the drawers, trashcan, but I couldn't find anything.

"Where am I?" I asked, and the room suddenly became chillingly eerie. "What's going on? Which department am I in? Let me think... which hospital department is the quietest?" I tried thinking of an answer, but nothing came to mind.

"I have to figure out where I am," I repeated nervously. Things were looking pretty bizarre. Where was the medical team? The visitors? I stared intently at the door, waiting for it to open, waiting for my chance to charge forward and seize whatever information I could to help me understand where I was. I needed answers. After all, what was happening here wasn't normal.

All I wanted was for someone to open the door, that was all. I didn't even care who, I just wanted someone to enter so I could get a bit of information.

Time seemed to crawl, but I kept my gaze straight at the door, alert and ready for it to open. "Just don't shut your eyes," I thought to myself, "just don't fall asleep." I forced myself to stay awake.

The day went by and morning turned to noon, noon to afternoon. "What's going on?" I asked confused. This didn't make sense, I'd been awake for hours, yet no one came to check on me. Didn't anyone care to see if I was breathing? Didn't they need to clean out my bowel movements? Didn't they need to check on my stats? Fever, blood pressure, something... "what was going on?"

I could see the sun setting outside the window, and as somber darkness engulfed the sky, I grew scared again. The fear of the night drove me nuts.

"I must stay awake," I desperately insisted, but I knew deep down that the chances of me succeeding were zero. Slowly, my eyes collapsed, and despite not wanting to fall asleep, my body had other plans in mind. I gave into the urge and dozed off, sinking deeper and deeper inward.

11.

I felt like I'd been asleep for hours on end, maybe even for a day or two. "How long was I out for?" I asked myself as I glanced around the room in confusion. It looked the same, except for one thing. I wasn't alone. Someone was here with me, here for a visit.

It was Talila. I looked at her for a few moments, to see what was different. It was her, but she didn't look the same. The smell of her sweet perfume was now a strong, spicy scent that filled the room. Her small brown eyes were covered in dark eyeshadow, making them look even smaller. This must have been my first time seeing her with makeup, it was weird. The color of her brown hair was now ginger, and she was wearing a tight black dress, buttons running along its length, something I never pictured seeing her in.

If only I could talk, I'd ask her, "Which horror movie did you come out of?" I chuckled. "At least I still have my sense of humor."

Her slow, heavy gestures looked weird, compared to her normally swift behavior. What was I missing here... I struggled to understand. I stared deeply into her eyes to try and make some sense of this chaos, but I couldn't find any answers. It felt like crashing into a brick wall.

Her eyes scrutinized my body, looking for any signs of life, like my mom used to do. She seemed worried, and after several long minutes of examining me from every possible angle, and receiving nothing in return, she sat down restlessly on my bed, her back facing me, and stared out the window.

"This is my last visit here," she stated quietly and folded her hands on her stomach. "I'm sure you understand."

Actually, no, I couldn't understand anything. We'd met the day before the surgery and spent the whole night talking and laughing like two idiots. And now what? What had happened in the gap between then and now?

I lay there like a useless fossil. I was there physically, but my body was completely deactivated. If, before the surgery, I was paralyzed from the neck down, now my whole body was in a vegetative state. I could hear and see, but I couldn't talk or move my face.

"I hope you won't be mad," she said, with her back to me. "I'm sure you understand... everything here has changed. We've all moved on, all of us. Only you've stayed the same, always the same." She sighed in desperation. "I dyed my hair orange, you see." She turned to me and crouched down, letting the strands of her hair tickle my face. She kissed me delicately on the forehead like she was my aunt or something.

"Hey, I'm not dead yet!" I wanted to yell. "Save your aunty kisses for someone else!" But I couldn't say a word.

"I thought," she whispered, nuzzling up closer to my face. "That maybe if you'd see the change I did to my hair, it would help you... you know... wake up. Get it?" She pinched my cheeks with force, but I couldn't feel a thing. "But then

I realized it was just another one of my crazy ideas to help you wake up. Maybe I'm being childish. Everyone says orange hair suits me." Talila forced out a smile and fluttered her eyelashes.

"Everyone's talking about my hair color, it's ridiculous. They're all saying how pretty I look with it, but between us, who cares? Why do people always care for the stupidest things? I did it for you, only for you. I thought that maybe... if I'd pull off such a radical thing, it would help you... you know, come back. But they... everyone, they have no idea I did it for you. They don't really know me too well, but that's okay. I'm not mad."

A silence lingered, only to be broken by the ring of Talila's phone. She got up and snatched it from her bag. Looking at the screen, she instantly ended the call.

"You'll be happy to hear I opened my own studio. I traveled to India by myself and returned with all the fabric I dreamed of having years ago. I sew my own purses now, I even have my own online shop. People are ordering like crazy, you won't believe it! Here, look." She flipped her phone around and showed me her online store, scrolling down so I'd see all her products.

"It's going pretty well, there's a real demand for my bags," she said proudly and put down her phone. She took a cigarette out of her bag, lit it, and approached the window, dragging on it slowly as she leaned on the windowsill and peered out.

I was surprised. Since when did Talila smoke? The way she moved, and how she talked to me... it was all so different, completely different from how I remembered her.

"What's happening here?" I tried to figure out what was

going on. "Think fast!" I urged myself. "What, what is she really telling you all this for? Use your head and think!" I felt like I was on a fast train that was speeding forward and about to crash into another one charging straight ahead. My brain felt like it had stopped working.

Suddenly, Talila's phone rang again. She put out her cigarette in the sink, returned to sit on my bed, and picked up the call.

I didn't listen to her conversation, I just looked at her, desperately trying to get her to see that I was here, that I could hear and see her. But it was futile. My body wasn't reacting to the instructions I gave it.

Talila finished talking and put her phone down on the bedside table. I knew this was my chance to get some information. I focused all of my energy on the task, and after one split second, I managed to do it. It was just a number, just a number shining on a screen, but that number said it all. I was stunned, I couldn't believe my eyes. The date on the screen exposed the cold, hard truth, connecting all the dots. Now, it was clear to me: that long, endless night had blurred into a lot more than that, into a timeless sphere. The incessant stillness in the room, and Talila, who now looked so different. Who would let an eighteen-year-old fly to India on her own to get some fabric? Who? Really, who?

"What a fucking idiot!" I told myself angrily. "Maybe someone whose daughter isn't fucking eighteen anymore! Someone whose daughter graduated high school years ago?!"

At that moment, all I felt was a disorienting dizziness and overwhelming nausea. It hit me all at once. I could now see that her odd behavior, as well as the clothes she wore, the cigarette she smoked, and the business she raved about, all came together to form one harsh answer I wasn't able to accept.

"This can't be," I told myself. "Where have I been all this time?" I was scared to do the math, but it was inevitable. A brief calculation gave way to a terrifying truth—I'd been this way for five years and three days. The day of the surgery was exactly five years and three days ago.

"Did I tell you that I hung your photo in my studio, a six-foot by six-foot image? Everyone says I'm crazy for hanging such a huge picture of you, and in the middle of the studio no less. When customers ask me who you are, I immediately say you're some idiot I once knew. I'm not in the mood to tell stories and collect pitiful looks. You know me, I was born with zero tolerance for people, save for a few." She pinched me on the cheek again, lit a new cigarette, and placed her head on my chest.

"Do you want some?" she asked and tried to push the cigarette between my lips, but it was obviously useless. She eventually gave up the idea.

"Oh well, you never liked cigarettes anyway." She smiled. "Just between us..." She inhaled the smoke into her lungs and slowly released it from her lips. "They're right. I'm really crazy. I talk to you sometimes, to your picture. Sometimes I curse, sometimes I just talk to tell you what's been going on with me, maybe ask for your advice. I like having you around. My mom thinks I've lost it. That's also the reason I came here today. She took me to a shrink, and after a few meetings with him, we agreed that I should take your picture out of my studio. He said I must put an end to this, and that the best thing for me would be to stop visiting you here at the hospital. He believes it's totally unnecessary. Can you believe him? Unnecessary..." Talila laughed and gave me a firm kiss on the lips.

"If only you could react, it would make things easier, you know," she whispered. I could sense the anger in her voice. She walked over to the window, opened it, and flicked out the cigarette.

"The thing is, last week, when I talked to you at the studio, Well, more like yelled at you for the thousandth time, my mom walked in on me. 'Who are you talking to?' she asked, even though she knew the answer. I could see the fear in her eyes. That's it, her daughter had officially gone mad. Here she is, yelling and talking to a picture in a room as if it was a real human being. She's insane. Her hands trembled, and she said I'd gone nuts and that it was time for me to seek help.

"At first, I was mad, how dare she? But I knew she was right. And a few days later, I decided that I had to put an end to this. I took down your picture and gave it to her. I think she hid it in our attic, somewhere I can't reach it. She promised she wouldn't throw it away, and I believe her. But now, I also need to stop coming to the hospital." Talila grew silent and took a deep breath in like gasping for air.

I felt sorry for everything she was going through, I wanted to yell at her to stop listening to everyone around her, that I was here now, that I'd come back, that I could hear her every word. That I'd do everything to stay here, that I could've given up a long time ago, given into the voices and left, but I was here. I still hadn't given up.

"Mom's waiting for me outside." Talila walked to the sink. She washed her face and let the water roll slowly off her skin.

"I promised myself I wouldn't cry, and I'm going to

keep that promise," she said confidently as she looked at her wet face in the mirror.

"Okay, I'll get going now. I'm just going to go, without kissing you, or hugging, or sniffing. That's it, this is over. I have to go. I have to do this. I'll just walk out of the door and leave," she rambled, encouraging herself as she stared at her face for a few final moments.

Finally, she picked up her bag, tossed her phone inside, and walked to the door. She stood close to the entrance with her back facing me. "You can do this!" she insisted.

"Come on, get out of here already!" She slowly placed her hand on the door handle, and after a long minute, pushed it down until it finally creaked open.

I managed to spot her mom in the hall waiting for her. She opened the door and reached her hand out to Talila to help her out. They looked at each other without saying a word. All Talila had to do was take one more step, and she'd be out of the room. It wasn't easy for her, and it took a few more minutes, but she finally did it. She stepped outside and collapsed on her mom, into her warm embrace.

"Let's go?" her mom said as she stroked Talila's face.

"Let's go," Talila barely responded, her voice sounded like she was choking. She had to force herself to complete the task she had come here for. She released her grip from the door handle and the door slammed forcefully behind her.

I felt a sense of emptiness fused with fear. All I wanted was to shut my eyes and sleep, to escape this horrible reality I'd woken into. But I was afraid to shut my eyes again and disappear for another five years... who would visit me then? Maybe just my mom and dad, once a month, every two months, just to feel good about themselves.

I closed my eyes for just a few short moments, but rapidly dove back to that place, where the voices spoke to me from all corners, tugging at me forcefully. "Just don't fall asleep. You can't..." I told myself and opened my eyes again.

I knew that in my current state, I was bound to crack easily, give up, and give in to their strong pull. I was bound to follow them into the place they desperately wanted to take me to.

I was mentally broken. New thoughts sprung to mind. "Why am I trying this hard? Maybe the best thing to do would be to let go and stop fighting them." I felt completely empty by this point, drained. All of a sudden, my incessant war against these voices seemed entirely irrational.

12.

Conversation No. 4 Between Me and "My Bro"

- I can see you're fighting.

- Fighting?

- Yes, to stay here.

- You mean against the voices?

- Voices?

- Isn't that what they are?

- They're a lot more than "voices," you're the one who decided to just listen to them. They're guardian angels, and they have a mission for you. They won't give up.

- Angels? I thought angels were supposed to be good, so why are they scaring me? I asked disappointed.

- The angels? Scary? Not at all! You're the one who's afraid of joining them, of crossing over to the other side.

- Of course I'm afraid. Why wouldn't I be? I don't want to leave. Who knows what's waiting for me there? I'd rather stay here, I replied firmly.

- You have nothing to fear!

- Great, that's easy for you to say. You're high up in the sky, but for us, the little people down here, the little dots you see from above, it's scary! We were told all our lives to fear death, and between us, I don't think heaven is waiting for a guy like me, with all the shit I did in life... with my arrogance and stuff. I think I'm heading straight to hell, aren't I?!

- No.

- Are you sure?

- I'm sure. The thing is, you've been holding onto this "heaven and hell" idea for many incarnations. It's been going on for a long time. You're better off letting go of those ideas once and for all. I assure you, they're not real.

- Really? There's no such thing as hell?

- No.

- I've always pictured hell as some scorching, muggy, stinky place.

- Look, there's room to "pay for your sins" but it's not the hell you have in mind. It's not a place full of evil and suffering. Much like there's room for "enjoying" the kind deeds you did, but again, it's not some heaven with chirping birds everywhere.

- Really... I was quite impressed.

- Yes, really. It's important to understand that the world beyond is different than the one here.

- Different, how?

- Everything is out in plain sight, exposed, and shared by all. Everyone can read each other's thoughts, everyone knows what the other feels, it's an open system.

- You don't say!

- Yes. It's the opposite of the world down here, where everyone keeps their thoughts, feelings, and intentions to themselves.

- Wow, it sounds like there's nowhere to hide there.

- True, but there's no need to hide as well. Everyone there knows what is most important!

- Which is...?

- You tell me

- I ..... don't.... know... I stuttered. I know what's most important for people here in this world. You know, money, success, power, and stuff.

- So it's exactly the opposite up there. Those at the top of the pyramid are those with the most love for others. Over there, the more one gives freely, the more one loves unconditionally, the higher up the pyramid one climbs.

- In other words, they're suckers. I laughed.

- Not at all.

- I'm kidding.

- This isn't funny.

- Okay, okay, I just felt like I needed to laugh a bit with all this seriousness.

- This is a serious matter.

- Okay, I got you, sorry.

- Unconditional love and genuine altruism, without any expectation of getting something back, determines your rating in the next world.

- I get it. So, in my case, I'm heading straight to the bottom of the pyramid, right? People like me... who spend all their lives focusing on themselves, arrive at this place and are sent to the bottom in a matter of seconds, yeah? I asked and waited for His response. He didn't say anything, so I continued.

- Between us, what did I actually do here on Earth? All seventeen years of my life? All I did was obsess over myself, have fun, and party. The only thing I cared about was feeling good about myself. I'm sure you don't get many points up there for self-love, right?

- Your striving for success is much appreciated, as well as your need for having fun. However, up there, how you treated the other is far more important.

- If so, my situation is shitty, right? Not good at all, nope... I get it. I'll be sent straight to the bottom of the pyramid, won't I?

I felt sorry for myself at this point. He didn't reply, and we were quiet for a while.

- Frankly speaking, bro, I don't even remember when I last gave someone something, just because I felt like it. Everything was always about interests, seemingly "healthy" ones. At the end of the day, it was all about what I wanted to achieve. Okay, I'm not the only one, yeah? Most people on Earth are like that, aren't they? Everyone is always thinking about what they can get out of the situation.

Again, He didn't reply, and we spent several long minutes in silence.

- Are you here? I finally asked, worried that He might have left already.

- Yes.

- Okay, honestly now, when I think about my life, about what I did, what I gave to who, I now realize that I gave the most to myself... are you with me? I asked impatiently.

- Yes.

- I loved myself the most. Unconditional love wasn't really my thing, not at all actually. I laughed, but couldn't help but feel bitter about it. I mean, yeah, sure, I showed love to the people around me, but everything was, you know... an exchange of some sort – love for love. Ahh... I sighed. I'm sure that the moment I cross to the other side, I'll be kicked down to the bottom. I'm sure no one will even look my way, right?! I asked and waited for His response. But, yet again, He didn't say a thing, He just went on with His annoying silent treatment. I was beginning to feel uncomfortable.

- Are you with me? I asked impatiently.

- I'm with you.

- Tell me, who is at the top of that pyramid of yours?

- Do you want names?

- No, no need. I'll find some myself. Wait... I began to run through a list of candidates in my mind. Oh! Yeah. I said after a few moments. Mother Teresa, right? And surely Gandhi, and Rabbi Nachman. People like that, right?

- Yes, them too.

- I'm sure thousands of people waited for them at the entrance

- Exactly!

- Oh... wait, I was joking. People actually waited to greet them?

- Why not? They deserve it. Over there, in the world beyond, there's no limit to the love one gives.

- Sure, sure, they deserve it. I smiled and imagined the thousands of people waiting for them at the entrance.

- More...

- What?

- Whatever you're picturing now in your head, imagine a lot more.

- What, you can see what I'm imagining?

- Yes.

- Amazing! So, how many more? Tens of thousands?

- More, a lot more.

- Hundreds of thousands?

- More.

- What, millions?

- Tens of millions. Whoever could greet them, came. But don't be mistaken, even "ordinary" people, those who weren't considered anything "special" in your world, have millions of people waiting for them at the entrance. There's no need for someone to be on the billboards of greatness. We know exactly who did what and who reached what rank. We know the exact greeting each soul deserves.

- Really? Impressive.

- Thank you.

- Say... I hesitated a bit before going on.

- Yes?

- This might sound a bit rude but, I need to know.

- Know what?

- How many? How many will be waiting for me at the entrance, when... you know, I get there?

- You'll have several people waiting for you.

- Yeah, I get that. But how many?

- You'll have people you've helped, those who've received your unconditional love, implicitly or explicitly, even if you don't remember it. Everything is about giving. Each loving act you did in this world counts, even if for you it wasn't anything serious. We note everything, it all counts.

- What? I asked, still quite confused. Even if I helped some old lady cross the street, that counts too?

- Do you find that insignificant?

- No, it's not that... it just doesn't seem like a big deal.

- For us it is, it's a huge deal. Particularly if you were giving only for the benefit of others, without expecting anything in return for it. Every good deed counts. Every loving act counts, we're serious.

- Everything counts?

- Yes.

- Even if it happened years ago?

- Yes, even if it happened many years ago, tens of years, we write it down. Nothing is forgotten.

- Okay, I get you. So I can officially say that my situation sucks. It sucks bad. Okay, I'm ready, talk to me. Give me numbers, how many? How many will be waiting for me at the entrance?

- I can see you really want to know.

- I do. So, come on, I'm listening... how many? One hundred people?

He didn't respond, so I went on.

- Fifty people? I asked and raised my voice a bit. How many? I asked again and waited anxiously for His answer.

- Well, what will it be? Should I go lower? Twenty people? I asked, growing more nervous by the second. What, am I that bad? My voice began to tremble.

- Do you have to know?

- Yes.

- Okay, I'll tell you, but just because you insist.

- Thank you.

- Three.

- Three? Are you kidding me? I recoiled in shame. Are you sure about that?

- I'm sure. Three. Three people.

I felt terrible. Not only was I crossing over to the world beyond, straight to the bottom of the pyramid with the world's most egotistical people, but I would also have no more than three people to walk me through it. I couldn't believe it. If only I could cover myself with a bed sheet, vanish, and end this talk. But I knew that was impossible. I was deeply entangled with nowhere to run. This wasn't in my hands anymore.

- You have nothing to be sorry for.

- Yeah, well, easy for you to say. You're not the one with three people greeting him at the entrance, are you!?

When He didn't reply, I began to guess who these three might be... if only I could ask Him who they were, but I couldn't. Gossiping always seemed pretty mediocre, not for me.

- I want you to know that the information you're getting here in this world means something. What I'm telling you now won't disappear, it's yours to keep. No matter when or how you decide to come back, the information I've shared with you will be available. It's yours forever.

- Great, and how exactly does this help me now?

- It will help you on your next journey, your next development.

- Meaning that... this won't help my current life?

He didn't respond.

- Wait, so what you're telling me now is that my life here is over? I'm done? I asked nervously. That these "voices," I'm sorry, "angels," have won? That I'm leaving?

Silence lingered in the room.

- Hey, bro, don't bail on me now. I want answers! I raised my voice. What exactly do you mean by "no matter when I come back to this world?" What are you trying to tell me? That this is the end for me?

- What about Talila? He asked, catching me off guard.

- What about her? I asked confused.

- Why did she come to say goodbye, why now?

- Why... because she said it's hard for her, and that she has to get away from me, that she's going mad, isn't that the reason?

- Yeah, but there might be another one.

- What do you mean?

- Maybe there's a reason you woke up five years and three days after the surgery...

- What do you mean?

- Think. I'm waiting.

- What is there to think about?

- There's no such thing as coincidence.

- Talila came to say goodbye just when I woke up. I woke up just now, and... wait. Suddenly, it hit me. Even though I didn't want to admit it.

- Is this the end for me? I asked fearfully. Am I understanding correctly? Is that it? Are they planning to cut me off, get rid of me? Did I wake up just to see my death, to witness my killing?

- Your release. Yes

- I can't believe this. They want to get rid of me?

- For them, you haven't been here for years already. You get it, right? You're a vegetable.

- Yes. I replied with sorrow. It's been a while. How did time fly so quickly, how can I not remember a thing?

I was upset by everything He told me, totally overwhelmed. Just don't fall, don't stop talking to Him. I was scared that He'd leave and I'd be left alone. The fear was paralyzing.

- I'm still trying to figure out the timeline. I really can't grasp that the surgery wasn't yesterday.

- No, it wasn't yesterday.

- Surely, after all these years, they don't believe I'll return, huh? So much time has passed. A year, and another... how much more can they take? Honestly, I get them. Come on, the most logical thing to do is to get rid of me, put me down and that's that.

- It was a joint decision. It took them years to get there.

- I'm sure, there's just one thing I don't understand...

- What?

- Why now? Why did I wake up now, right before they decide to pull the plug? What's the deal? I could've gone on sleeping and I wouldn't have felt a thing. I wouldn't have known anything about it. But why wake up now?

- Smart question.

- Thanks.

- I guess you could say you were given an opportunity. Life can change in a second.

- I don't understand.

- I think you do.

- Wait, what are you telling me? That this isn't over yet? Come on, be clearer, please. I'm begging. This is my life we're talking about! I was desperate.

- All you need is a response, even the tiniest of responses. Like a wink, a movement of the finger, or a sound. And that's it, they won't put you down.

- Okay.

- And for that to happen, you need a miracle.

- A miracle?

- Exactly, a miracle.

- But how? What? What can I do exactly? As you can

see, I'm trapped in this paralyzed body that doesn't exactly react to my orders.

- As I said, only a miracle can set you free. It's all up to you.

- No pressure at all... I laughed.

- Remember, every loving act counts. When the time comes, don't let it pass. Everyone makes mistakes, and everyone needs forgiveness, even the seemingly perfect people.

- What do you mean? Ugh, I'm totally confused. Can you be more accurate?

Once again, silence filled the room. And my biggest fear—Him leaving—happened. I was alone again.

Honestly, I was a bit offended that He would leave in the middle of our conversation. But I trusted His decision. It was probably the right time to end this conversation. I guess there wasn't much left to say, and I'd already received precisely what I needed from Him, not more.

I knew I had to act quickly, that I was running out of time. I needed to be super focused to not miss out on this miracle He mentioned. Time wasn't on my side. I woke up now because I received a rare opportunity to fight for my life, just before they put me down for good.

"I have to stay focused, I can't miss out on my last chance," I repeated to myself again and again. However, my mind quickly spiraled into thoughts about the three people waiting for me at the entrance. I repeatedly went over the people I met throughout my life: kindergarten, school, basketball, my extended family, my friends, and neighbors. I went over hundreds, maybe thousands of faces. Who could these three be?

I couldn't let it go, I was too curious. Maybe I had to

know who they were because the number was so low. I tried recalling the kind deeds I'd done, the love I gave without any expectation of getting back, but sadly, I couldn't come up with anything. Every time I searched for it, I dived deeper into my thoughts, until it felt like I was sinking into quicksand. Because the truth of the matter was, I was a freaking egomaniac, a little shit who only cared for himself. Honestly, if I ever did something for someone, it was only to get something out of it, only because it served some cause I was after, that's all.

After hours of searching, I came up empty-handed. I completely gave up and felt incredibly bad about it. I felt even worse than before, probably because I had no idea who those three were.

"Who am I?" I asked myself. "What kind of person would I be in this world, without a surfboard, without basketball, without Talila, without my parents, without my friends? I would be nothing, an egotistical creature who cares only for his interests and cravings, from the moment he wakes up to the moment he falls asleep, every day, all over again."

Suddenly, out of nowhere, I thought of Fanny, who had cared for me in the previous department before the surgery. I thought of how she'd always sing songs in Spanish to me, talk, smile, and stroke my face.

"Fanny the nurse." It suddenly dawned on me. Now, I saw her in completely different lighting. She wasn't just my favorite nurse who came to do her job. It was now clear as daylight—Fanny had secured herself a high spot up there in the pyramid of the world beyond. She surely wouldn't find herself at the bottom with someone like me. She wouldn't be greeted by three people, three people she didn't even know. She'd probably be greeted by hundreds, maybe even thousands. And she'd know every single one of them. She'd recognize them all. That's for sure.

I thought about the fact that I always tried to be different from others. The most important thing in my mind was to take care of myself, of my honor, and I didn't always play nice to get there. All I cared about was not being a loser. I always chose the wittiest sentences, just to take down those around me, with no sympathy whatsoever.

Honestly, I didn't care if I hurt them, the only thing I cared about was keeping them away. I can think of numerous occasions I left people feeling embarrassed and confused by my shameless, snappy comments. They stood mute without any chance of responding back. They were too busy trying to process what I'd said. I loved seeing that startled look on their faces, and their incapacity to respond. This sounds horrible, I know, but for some reason, this had always satisfied me. I loved feeling like they were beneath me, that I managed to bury them deep underground. It always made me happy. Here, I won again! I'm smarter and faster than them. I've left them behind to eat dirt.

Fanny always gave me the feeling she actually cared about me, unlike the other nurses and medical staff. She always saw me for who I was, even though I was kind of half-dead.

I remember when my parents came for a visit one day, and she was in the room with us. Neither of them glanced her way. That's how my parents are. They speak only to the doctors in the department. Both my parents are academics with a Ph.D., and they choose to speak with those at "their level." Those beneath them don't matter. The condescending way they look at people instantly gives them away. I also had that look, I also chose to be with those I felt were at my level, or at least near it. Everyone else didn't exist for me and weren't worthy of my attention. They were like air. Yeah, that's what they were. Air, nothing more.

I loved the touch of Fanny's hand on my face. Mom, Talila, and Aunt Esther also stroked my face when they visited, but Fanny's hands were something else. They belonged to a woman who didn't know me before the crash, a woman who viewed me just as I was, a lifeless clump of meat lying on a bed with stinky bedsores. Despite all of that, she decided to grant me unconditional love and genuine warmth, even though she really didn't need to.

I don't remember receiving this "free love" at home. To love without any particular reason wasn't something we did. Love was always about my achievements. I can recall a warm embrace the day I was chosen as the head of the student body, or a kiss on the cheek whenever I scored an A+ on my test. That's how it was at home: if you deliver results—you get love. You could say that love for us was a limited resource. You want some? You have to work hard for it! Thinking about it now, it's a pretty weird situation for a single child to be in...

My parents' visits to the hospital before the surgery were always "on the way." My mom always visited me in the morning on her way to work, and my dad always visited me whenever he had an opening in his schedule, or on his way to the airport. I was always happy to see them, but deep down, I longed for them to visit when they weren't "on their way." I would even prefer that they come less, but that they come, really come, to see me. Simple as that. Not on their way to... on their way from... I wanted them to sit with me and talk, without having to rush anywhere. I wanted them to forget the world outside, that's how I believe it should be. I feel sorry for my parents. I'm sure that all those years of having me lie here have been a burden. I surely fucked up their lives. Frankly, I'm nothing more than a big boulder that dropped from the sky out of nowhere and is now blocking their chances of moving forward toward their goals.

I know the truth. I know that if they could, they would choose not to visit me at all. I can understand. I'm sure it's tough, not only because of my paralysis but also because they don't know the reason behind it all. This probably drives them nuts. They can't grasp why I would do such a stupid trick like the Anaconda. Why I would risk my life when all odds were against me? This move of my mine is lightyears away from their sterile, organized way of living. I think they'll never understand the reason behind my crash.

13.

Tomer entered the room and sat by my bed with a smile on his face.

"Hey dumbass." He shook my lifeless hand as if I was awake. It looked like he was really happy to see me.

"Well, still causing trouble around here?" He let go of my hand and placed it gently on the bed. Looking at him, I could barely recognize the guy. He seemed so different, much more like a man than a boy. He had a black beard and long hair that fell below his shoulders. The clothes he wore were an obvious sign that it had been a while since we last met, and no matter how much I tried to ignore it, I felt jealous, yes, jealous. I felt a slight pinching in my heart as if a large pincer was gripping me tightly.

Tomer wore purple harem pants and a white, loose linen shirt. Around his neck hung a red beaded necklace. Never in my life would I have pictured him wearing such a thing, specifically that loose, open shirt. Wow, now that I was looking at him, he seemed so different. This wasn't the Tomer I knew. Not only did he look different, but his whole "vibe" was different, something else.

"Well, what's up?" he asked and looked at me as if

waiting for an answer.

I was pretty surprised to see him here. Maybe he knew I'd returned? I felt hopeful.

"I know you," he said. "You won't give up. You hate giving up, don't you?!" He scooted back on the chair and leaned his head on my bed, glaring at me for several long seconds, trying to piece his thoughts together.

If only I could let him know somehow that I was here, right here, listening to him, seeing him... it would've been perfect.

"In the Far East, you're taught to choose your words wisely," he said and shut his eyes for a moment to center himself.

After a minute or so, he opened them and continued. "Well, where to begin... it's been so long, maybe I'll tell you about my trip to the Far East. I'm sure you'll like that... it's kind of weird to summarize such a huge thing, after all, I was away for a year. So many things have happened, but just so you know, you little dumbass, I thought about you a lot over there. Don't go on thinking that this crash of yours only affected you. We were all affected by it, all of us got screwed. Because of you, my parents forced me to take a satellite phone with me on the trip. What a nightmare, huh? I had to take it everywhere, so freaking annoying. So thanks man, really, thanks." He laughed. "I flew with the guys, it was obvious we'd go together. I was the last to finish the army. I became an officer, man. Don't look at me like that, you know me, always taking it to the extreme." He smiled and brushed my hair back. "So much hair, you're going for the savage look huh," he laughed and tucked a few strands behind my ears. "Ahh, now I can see your face." He leaned back, satisfied with himself. "Okay, where was I ... ah! So the whole gang waited for me. I worked for about half a year until I collected enough money, working as a surfing guide with kids throughout the summer. Those little guys drove me nuts, it was a nightmare. They're freaking spoiled man, I'm telling you, those kids, they let themselves do whatever. Little shits. Wait, where was I...what was I talking about? Oh, yeah. So, after six months, I had enough money to travel. We flew to Thailand. We were so pumped! I even remember we talked about you on the flight, everyone said you would've joined us if not for the crash. But I disagreed. I know you, I don't think you would've come. Right? Am I right? Would you have come? I don't think you would've left your Talila behind for so long, right?" he asked. It felt like he was really expecting a response.

"Okay, so the moment we landed in Bangkok, in less than a day, I realized I was fucked. Apparently, the only reason the gang went on this trip was to do drugs. I told them to chill out, but no one listened. It was all they cared about. And the moment they found a dealer... wow... that's when the real party started. You can't imagine the quantities... they took everything. What can I say... I looked at them from the side and couldn't believe this was actually happening. You know me, I don't deal with that shit. I told myself, 'Okay Tomer, let it go. You're not their dad. Give them a few days to have fun, they'll be back to normal soon.'

"So I decided to head out north on my own, leaving them behind for a few days. 'By the time you get back they'll be over it,' I told myself. Well... as it turns out, no." Tomer sighed. "You won't believe what I returned to. These guys, man, they're insane... I was wrong. The party had just begun. They hit rock bottom, diving all the way down. They smoked and drank like crazy. They laughed, cried, talked like idiots, got into fights and even went to hookers. I kept thinking this was the lowest they could get, but they went even lower. And the following day—even lower. It turns out, man, once you hit rock bottom, you run into a lot of swerving steps," he spoke quietly, a tinge of sadness in his voice.

"Come to think of it, I'm ashamed of them. It's probably a good thing you weren't there to witness that mess. I tried talking to them, snapping them out of it, but nothing helped. Some of them, as you can probably guess, were commanders in the army, officers. They had responsibilities, soldiers to take care of. I really couldn't believe what I was seeing. 'You fucking idiots, we're on our epic trip, the trip of a lifetime, and this is what you're doing? Look at yourselves. After three freaking years in the army, this is what you've decided to do all day?' I yelled at them. I was furious, but they really didn't care. They even found it funny to see me acting like a responsible grownup. They didn't listen. 'Get a move on, bro,' they told me. 'You're ruining it for everyone.' Needless to say, I eventually cracked, and after two and a half weeks, I split.

"I planned on disappearing from their sight for a week, and then returning to find them, hopefully sane and back to their old selves. But the moment I went out in nature on my own, I realized that there was no going back. I decided to travel alone, alone felt the best. Look, it wasn't easy at first. I felt a bit bad about the guys, but I realized that the farther away I was from them, the better I felt... day after day, I began to loosen up. I felt free, happy with being alone. As it turns out, the best thing for me was to travel on my own. After Thailand, I flew to Nepal where I went hiking in the mountains all on my own. I could've joined a group of Israelis I met there, but I didn't want to. I wanted to be alone, just by myself, in that incredible nature. How can I explain… it felt like entering another dimension, a whole new world, like being reborn. Suddenly, I stepped out of the Israeli bubble I grew up in, and inside an entirely different bubble, a better one, calmer and saner." Tomer got up from his chair and walked back and forth around the room.

"I walked by myself in the mountains for weeks. Sounds crazy, right? Yeah, it wasn't always easy, I was afraid at times. And yeah, I'm not going to lie to you, Mr. Fearless, there were some rough nights. Just me and myself out there, with no one around. I was scared to death at times, but I pushed through. I didn't want to be controlled by fear. 'Think like Yair!' I kept telling myself, 'Pretend you're Yair,' that's honestly what I said. You were never afraid of anything... that killed me, man. Between us, you're my true master. Really."

He sat back down and inhaled deeply. "Ah…" He sighed. "If only you could've been there with me… I needed you up there in the mountains. It would've been fun, that's for sure. Well, from Nepal I traveled to Hong Kong, India, Burma, and China… it was incredible, really. I did the whole trip by myself, a full year on my own. I could've joined the people I met along the way, but I didn't want to lose my balance. I felt that my 'real journey' had to be done solo. And don't get me wrong, it sucked at times. I was robbed, sick, suffered days of true loneliness, I even began talking to myself, I might've lost it at one point." He laughed to himself. "But between us, I was happy, truly happy, the happiest I'd ever been in my life." Tomer looked out the window in silence.

"I thought about you countless times during the trip. I felt like it was your journey too. Listen, bro, if you'd joined, it would've been perfect. Really, I would've given up the whole alone thing if you had come along. It would've been just the two of us. We probably would've fought over who has the smelliest socks, and you probably would've devoured every chocolate bar we'd get 'because it was too yummy,' like you always did, you idiot," he smiled at me. "But other than that, I think we would've gotten along perfectly, right?!" He stopped talking and crouched down to get a colorful beaded bracelet out of his bag. He placed it on my wrist and looked at me for several moments, pleased with himself.

"Well, what do you say? It's nice, isn't it? It's your bracelet of hope, containing all the colors of the rainbow. You dumbass, look at what I brought for you, all the way from China." He glanced at the bracelet. "Sweet, I really do have great taste." He rested my hand on the bed and smiled to himself.

"Sometimes, I think about the call you gave me the night of the crash. I couldn't pick up. What did you want to tell me? I keep having these 'what if…' thoughts," he said sadly and took a deep breath in.

"If only I answered the phone, maybe all of this wouldn't have happened. Hmm? Why did you go back to the field? Weren't you supposed to be home studying after the game? Why did you go back? When I saw you out there again, you looked a bit spaced out. I even remember asking you something, but you answered 'later.' Were you really planning on telling me? Or were you just trying to get rid of me?" Tomer asked and looked deep into my eyes, longing for answer.

After a few moments of silence, he went on. "Don't get me wrong, I replayed your crash again and again in my mind, hundreds of times. I tried to figure out what exactly happened. What was I missing? How did we let you do that trick? What were we thinking? All of us, me and that stupid gang of ours... we just stood there on the opposite hill and let you do it. We let you do the anaconda trick we knew you had no chance of actually pulling off. How didn't we stop you? You know what? Forget them, I don't care about them. How didn't I stop you? Your best friend... I didn't stop you. How didn't I punch you or something? How didn't I toss your bike down the hill? What was up with me? How did I just sit there on the hill and let it happen? Maybe, like the rest of the gang, I didn't really believe you would do it. I remember being curious about whether you'd actually pull it off. Where was my common sense at the time? I have no idea man." He rubbed his hand over his face then crossed his hands over his stomach.

"Just so you know, I hate myself for that. I'm the only from the gang who knew something had happened. I knew you were in a place you shouldn't be, I noticed you were acting weirdly, I was the only person who was supposed to stop you, but I didn't. I just joined the gang on the hill to watch the show unfold, the show of my best friend crashing into the abyss."

Tomer stopped rambling and got up furiously, the impact of his gesture caused his chair to topple backward. He walked to the window, leaned his hands on the glass, and pressed his head firmly against the window.

"I've been having this recurring dream for several years now, where I try to stop you from falling, but I never succeed. I already know what's going to happen in the dream, and even though I do everything I can to block your way, you always manage to escape and do that fucking stunt of yours." Tomer moved away from the window and began pacing the room nervously.

"What was the deal? What happened? Why didn't you tell me? I'm your best friend. We've been friends since kindergarten, you idiot. I know everything about you, why did you do it? How did this even happen? I remember you guys won the game and got into the finals. Everyone said you were super stoked, that you killed it on the court, so what exactly happened?" Tomer raised his voice and stood above me, a mad expression on his face.

"Well, answer me!" he yelled, and it seemed like he genuinely expected to receive a response. "Do you get that this is driving me insane? That I can't let it go? I can't put it all together, something is missing!"

A few moments later, Tomer picked up the chair from the floor and sat by my bed again. "I even thought I'd find the answer to your crash in your room, so one day, I asked your parents for permission to go in. I told them I really missed you. They let me enter alone, so I let myself go through your drawers and closets. Man, you're really tidy." He smirked. "You could've been a great pharmacist. But no, I didn't find anything, just love songs you wrote for Talila. Pretty good ones, I have to say, a bit cheesy, but you got some real talent man." The door suddenly opened and Tomer grew quiet.

Mom and Dad entered and recognized him straight away. He got up quickly, walked over, and gave them a big hug.

They talked for a few moments, then recoiled in silence. They looked back and stared at me as if I was some fish in an aquarium. Seeing the desperation in their eyes, I felt embarrassed. I knew they were all searching for some sign of life, the smallest sign just to prove I still existed. I wished I could do something, but my body stayed as it was, like a shitty statue. I felt awful about it.

Finally, Tomer broke the silence and said he had to go. He said goodbye to my parents and leaned closer to me with a smile on his face. He then whispered into my ear, "Don't be afraid, it's not over until it's over!" I looked at him in shock. He got up, turned around, and left the room.

I spent several long minutes glaring at the bracelet he gave me. "It's just a bracelet," I told myself, yet this colorful thing managed to light up this gray room with its vibrant colors. "Maybe this bracelet was a sign of hope… Yeah, sure, just don't get your hopes up too much," I told myself. There was no need for foolish, wishful thinking.

"After all, it looks like I've become some 'holy site' for people to visit. The cold, hard truth is that they're all here to say goodbye. First Talila, then Tomer, and now my parents… that's it, it's pretty obvious what's happening here. My time is running out."

Tomer's visit really moved me, I missed the guy. If only I could talk to him, ugh, that would've been awesome. The moment he left, I felt my heart sink. I dived right back into self-pity. I really didn't want to go there. Now that I didn't have much time left, I knew I couldn't afford dwelling on it.

"Just get over your feelings, you're stronger than them," I told myself. Funnily, this wasn't even my sentence, it was my dad's. Dad has always tried to lecture me about his theory of emotions. He treats emotions like some annoying fly buzzing around the room. According to him, only the weak let emotions control them. According to Dad, a life governed by emotions is a wasted one. "Emotions are always in motion, they don't rest for a minute," he explained. "Sometimes you're sad, sometimes depressed, happy at times. But that's all there is to it. It's all temporary, just like the weather, in constant flux. It's not like you wake up one morning and decide not to brush your teeth because it's cloudy, not sunny like you thought it would be, right? The same goes for transient emotions. They come and go. They change in a matter of seconds or minutes. You're better off focusing on your goals instead of dwelling on your emotions," dad would explain to anyone willing to listen. According to him, the one thing important in life was to focus on one's goals. That's all that mattered.

"Only the weak let emotions control them, and emotions will do nothing but take you down, all the way down. If there's an important goal in mind, it'll exist the following morning too, unlike emotions, that come and go uncontrollably."

I knew I was thinking just like Dad now, and that I had no other choice but to get over these overwhelming emotions.

When Tomer talked about his trip, I felt like I was really there with him. I imagined us on the snowy mountains, staring out at the wild nature, ahh... the joy. I held onto my imaginative images, stuffed them in tight little packages, and stored them deep in my memory. What else was there to do? I could never afford to go on a trip like that in my state. This would always be nothing but a dream for me. Even if I was in a wheelchair, I still wouldn't have gone on a trip like that. Being handicapped? No way. I wouldn't have my friends pushing me up the mountain. I wouldn't agree to get my picture taken like the "cute little handicapped guy who conquered the mountain in his fucking wheelchair." Nope, not for me. This whole thing just doesn't suit me. I imagined myself reaching the summit and taking a photo with everyone. I could easily picture some eager news broadcaster joining us and documenting my emotional journey across the Nepalese mountain. The news editor would make sure to broadcast the piece right at the end of the show, so viewers could wrap up the bad news with a smile, just like producers like to do.

I hate the thought of being that corny entertainer. I didn't want to be the guy in a wheelchair at the summit. I didn't want to be asked by a reporter, "So, how do you feel?" And to respond with excitement, "I feel great. I fulfilled a dream of mine with the help of my fantastic friends who pushed my heavy wheelchair up the mountain. I'm so proud of them." Nope, this isn't like me at all.

I could picture Mom and Dad turning it into a huge deal, inviting all their friends, opening fancy bottles of wine, and gathering around the TV together. "What a remarkable child," they'd all say, and forget for a moment that I'm fucking handicapped.

Dad would pour wine for everyone. "Ah… my incredible child has done the impossible." He would raise his glass in the air and everyone would cheer together. Mom would tear up, and everyone would be delighted: my friends, parents, the reporter, the editor, the producer, and, of course, the people at home. Yes, everyone would be happy, everyone except me, the one who agreed to act as their "crippled pet." I can't let something like this happen to me. This isn't like me at all.

14.

Tomer walked out, leaving Mom and Dad alone in the room. One look at them was enough to know that today would probably be my last one. Soon I'd be gone, maybe even in the next hour. Words aren't always needed to realize something big is about to happen. The dark circles under Mom's eyes highlighted how little sleep she'd been getting all these nights. She looked lost, unable to fix her gaze on me as she drifted around the room. Dad, on the other hand, stood by the window and peered out, like searching for something or someone.

Finally, Mom sat by my bed and stroked my hair. "All these years, and you look the same," she stated as she carefully scanned my face. "My beautiful boy." She traced her hand on my face and hair. A tear slid down her cheek, and she rapidly wiped it away, glancing over at Dad who stood with his back to her.

"Time to say goodbye, I promised myself I wouldn't cry," she whispered. "Dad and I promised to be strong, we promised we wouldn't get too emotional. We've come here to do what's right. You have to understand, it's been years. There's no point in dragging this out any longer. We've decided to donate your organs." She sobbed. "It's important we do something good with your body, help others, save lives."

She stared at me intently, taking in every bit of my frozen face. Dad turned to us and looked at me, but from afar. He kept silent. The sorrow on his face ran deep.

Three nurses entered the room and greeted my parents. Mom got up from the bed and stood next to Dad by the window. The nurses then began treating me. They removed the bed sheet from my body and inspected me thoroughly, typing on the computer as they went.

A few minutes later, a doctor entered the room and scrolled through the data they'd collected. My heart beat fast. "That's it, I'm done!" I told myself. "Are these how the last minutes of my life are going to look?" I asked in despair. I couldn't believe this was happening to me. If only I could scream or kick. Instead, my body just lay there, rooted, without any movement. I felt an immense sense of agony wash over me.

The examination took a while, and through it all, Mom and Dad remained by the window. Mom was next to Dad, but she was facing him with her back. Suddenly, a terrifying thought crossed my mind. Maybe they hadn't agreed on this together? Maybe only one of them wanted to do this, and the other was simply dragged into it... if that was true, this was completely unfair. Wasn't this supposed to be a joint decision?!

"What do people think about before they leave this world?" I asked myself, but no answer came to mind.

"Okay, time to pull myself together!" I stressed. "In a matter of minutes, I'd be gone. Maybe I should just come to terms with it once and for all. This ends here... but no! I can't. I can't give up!"

The doctor announced that they were set and ready.

Mom and Dad hugged, Dad whispered something into Mom's ear and then asked everyone to leave the room because he wanted to say goodbye to me in private. In less than a minute, everyone left, everyone but the two of us.

Dad pulled in a chair and settled by my side. A tense silence filled the room. It appeared to be the last moments of my life, with Dad as my final witness.

I tried giving off a sign that I was still alive and breathing, that he shouldn't give up on me, that it was just my body that seemed lifeless. But I couldn't. How despairingly awful it was to see the angel of death take monster steps my way, while I lay helplessly without any way of escaping. My body didn't budge, not even an inch. It didn't listen to my orders. I was shut down from the outside, but raging from the inside. I felt seriously dizzy, and the notion of my impending death became impossible to bear.

What was most difficult was the fact that I lost, despite all of my struggles against the voices. Eventually, they were right. Things weren't under my control anymore. My parents were the ones deciding over my life, not me.

Dad seemed utterly nervous. Numerous new wrinkles were drawn on his aging face, and his black hair had now turned completely white. He seemed frazzled, searching for the right words to say. He looked at me every now and then, but nothing came out of his mouth.

I thought about how he sent the whole medical crew to wait outside the room until he finished talking to me. It suited him, having everyone work for him. It seemed that controlling his environment was something he simply couldn't help but do.

"They say you're not here anymore, that you haven't been

for years. They say you don't feel anything, that you're not suffering. We want to believe that's true. You see... your mom and I have met people who urgently need your organs. This will help them survive," Dad said quietly, his fingers shaking so badly that he folded them together. "We believe this is the right thing to do, to help, to give life. I really hope you're not here anymore, that you can't feel or hear me now. It's been five years, after all. Just the inescapable thought you might still be here is keeping me restless. What if..." He pushed his fist against his mouth, holding in his emotions. "Deep inside, I knew you were physically gone. Your brain is dead. But there's always room for doubt." He sighed, then lowered his gaze to the floor. "I know you're not here, but even if the chances are zero, there might be one speck of a chance that you can still hear me, so I have to share this with you before you go. You have to hear this, before we say goodbye." Dad stared at me for a second, then proceeded.

"We made it. You'll be happy to hear that my dream came true. It happened. This still feels surreal, but after fifteen years of hard work, we made it. Several pharmaceutical companies approached us, and we ended up choosing one. Now, our product will be marketed around the world. In spite of it all, we made it. Who would have believed that a random idea scribbled on a napkin at a café in Austria, on a snowy winter day, would one day turn into a real, life-saving medication? Millions of people from around the world are going to be cured of cancer. Even now, sharing this, I find it hard to believe that this is actually happening, that the medicine truly works. It wasn't easy, as you can imagine. After the development stage, we spent months arguing with greedy pharma companies that wanted nothing more than to make a profit, that completely forgot that we were dealing with sick people and that every day without the medicine mattered to them." Dad sighed.

"Well, despite the yearlong setback, we finally signed a contract, and the medicine will soon be marketed internationally. It's crazy how much ego, money, and power can hinder progress. I never loved politics." He stopped talking and leaned back on the chair. "Well look at me, rambling to myself... I want you to listen carefully to what I'm about to say. Every time I look at you, I wait for a response, some response: a wink, a finger movement, maybe even one direct glance my way, that's all, that's all I'm asking for. That will be enough for me to know you're here with me. If you can—do it, it will make me really happy." Dad focused his eyes on me for several minutes, and when he didn't get any response, he kept talking: "After purchasing our medicine, the pharma company arranged a huge event with journalists from all over the world, and the plan was for me to deliver a speech. The invited guests were colleagues, family, investors, and my research team... I have no words to describe how emotional I was. After all that I'd been through, this was the greatest moment of my life... I was officially making my mark on the world. I did it! I made it! The big day arrived, and the conference hall was full of people, photographers, and journalists. For a moment, I felt like I was at the Oscars, only instead of cinema-crazy fans, the crowd was full of cancer-ridden patients from all over the world. This ceremony would announce their chance at life again, that there may be a way to beat their cancer. It was important for me to talk specifically about the sick patients, the people themselves. They're the reason I set out on this journey in the first place. I wanted to remind all of those greedy, wealthy, corrupt pharma people that, eventually, we're dealing with human lives.

"Everyone clapped, and I remember that I smiled on my way to the stage. Some of my team members were already waiting for me on stage and waving hello. My paces were slow and measured, and my mind was going wild with excitement. I believe that was the first moment I genuinely processed what was happening, that despite all of the setbacks I'd been through these past fifteen years, I ended up achieving my goal."

Dad took in a deep breath and let out a sigh.

"On my way to the stage, I thought about my colleagues who accompanied me all these years, the few who stayed, and the many people who had joined me for a short period only to quit out of despair. I also thought of those who got in my way, who felt the need to tell me how insane I was at every opportunity they had, how useless and wasteful my project was. I thought about the exhausting and humiliating fundraising campaigns I carried out all those years, how hard it was, and how low I went just to keep things moving. I even thought of the 'forgotten lab technician' who, one night, mistakenly mixed the order of the test tubes and unintentionally caused a breakthrough in our research. Of course, she left the lab and insisted on how sorry she was for ruining our experiment, a mistake that cost us tens of thousands of dollars. In retrospect though, this little mistake led to our breakthrough. We managed to see what we couldn't beforehand. Who knows where we would've been today without that 'forgotten lab technician' whose name I have long forgotten." Dad stopped talking, then sat back on the chair near my bed and crossed his arms.

"I've spent years since your crash asking myself, again and again, why? I knew you perfectly well, or at least I thought so... even when you pushed yourself to the limit, even when you did extreme sports, you were always cautious. What exactly caused you to hover between two hills so far away from each other? What made you do such a reckless stunt? A stunt with zero chances of survival." Dad rubbed his face briskly until it grew red.

"From the moment this happened, this question has never once left my mind. It's always the same: why did you do what you did? It's the same question, over and over again, never letting me go. I want you to know that I interrogated your friends repeatedly, all of them, Talila as well. I even showed up at the field a few times to look into the stunt you did. Your friends told me that you had this inside joke going around, that if anyone wanted to end their lives, then the anaconda stunt would be a good fix. As a matter of fact, everyone knew it was a dangerous stunt. No one really thought of doing it, ever. Everyone knew that the chances of surviving it were zero. And you? Why would you risk yourself like that? Why would you want to do such a dangerous thing on the night of your basketball finals, a game I heard you nailed. I heard everyone saying you killed it out there! That you left the field happy and proud. So what? Huh? What is it? What am I missing here? This question has been on my mind for years. It's been keeping me awake at night. Why? Why? Your mom said that your friends weren't telling us the whole truth, that they probably knew something we didn't. Maybe they talked you into jumping, or maybe you felt so euphoric that night that you decided to pull it off and show everyone how much of a winner you are. But this didn't make any sense. This wasn't the answer. I know you, I know how cautious you always were. You would never risk it like that. And I know your friends, they're great kids, each one of them. They always agreed to talk with me, no matter how annoying I was or how many questions I had for them. No matter when or how I interrogated them, their answers were always the same. They were just as surprised you'd do something like that. They, too, couldn't understand why. What would make you storm out like that?"

Dad got up from the chair and paced back and forth across the room.

"These past few years... I became sad and withdrawn. Not only because we lost you, but also because I couldn't find the answer to this tormenting question. I even hired a private investigator, but he couldn't find anything either. The same question... over and over again, why? In bed, at the lab, on flights, on the chair in your empty bedroom. Why? I'm a bit embarrassed to say this, but sometimes, I felt like I was willing to give up my project, my life's work, just to get an answer. Just so I could finally sleep, and give my restless mind a break. On my visits here, I'd stare at you for hours in the hopes of finding some answer in your eyes, but that never happened."

Dad sat on the chair and pulled himself closer to the bed.

"I walked confidently to the stage, more excited than ever before. I remember feeling my pocket to make sure my speech notes were there, and at that very moment, I thought of you. I thought of how sad it was that you were not here to witness this huge moment. You'd surely be happy for me. After all, you're a huge part of this achievement. I want you to know that I appreciate your contribution, the patience to sustain all those days and nights I was missing, absent from your life, and all those games you invited me to but I couldn't make it, unlike the other dads. Today, I can see that I was entirely focused on my project, and you and Mom paid a high price for it. Even though you never complained and were always accepting, I know, deep down, that I failed."

Dad sighed and paused, staring into the air for a few moments.

"Where was I? Oh, yes. So I went on stage and started things off with a joke, a joke I'd rehearsed before. You know me, it was preplanned, I'm not naturally funny like you. Jokes aren't in my nature. But it worked, and everyone laughed. I took the speech out of my pocket and prepared to read. But at that very second, when I unfolded the paper after putting on my reading glasses, it happened, **boom**. **Suddenly**, out of the blue, without any prior thought, it hit me. Silence lingered in the hall, and everyone waited for me to speak, but I couldn't open my mouth. Do you get it? Yair, it happened. After all these years, I found it, the answer. The answer to the question that has never left my mind."

Dad got up from his chair, grabbed me by the shoulders, and began shaking my body from side to side.

"Do you get what I'm telling you?" he yelled and pulled me toward him forcefully as if he was urging me to get up.

"Are you listening to me? Are you?" He drew me closer and hugged me tightly. His body was shaking as tears rolled down his cheeks.

"It was right under my nose, it had been for years, but I completely overlooked it. Like sailing across the ocean to look for a treasure that is right in your backyard."

A few minutes later, Dad rested my body back on the bed, sat by my side with his back facing me, and breathed heavily.

"I look back at the moments before I went on stage. I was in the lobby with a few colleagues drinking cold champagne, laughing, for the one-hundredth time, about the 'forgotten lab technician' who fled because of her mistake, but actually helped kickstart this whole thing. What would we have done without that mistake of hers… 'Cheers! To the lab technician whose name we forgot.' We laughed and raised our glasses to the sky. 'Cheers to the invisible people,' one of my colleagues said.

"That's when it all started, where did I hear this saying before? 'Invisible people…' I asked myself. It caught my attention, but I couldn't dwell on it because we had to get in the hall. Only then, a second before I was to start my speech, it hit me. 'Invisible people' belonged to you. Yes, your task of saving the 'invisible people.' I breathed heavily and forced myself to read the first word from the page, but I couldn't.

"'A good boy you have,' I suddenly remembered the security guard, with his heavy Russian accent, who had been working in our building for years. After weeks of being away after your crash, I returned to work, and that was what he told me. I didn't understand what he wanted from me, so I walked right past this 'invisible person' and up the elevator. I didn't stop, not even for one second. I didn't realize that he had the answer.

"My collapse on stage was inevitable. All the dots I'd been trying to connect these past years came together in one dreadful moment. I couldn't handle it anymore. Why would a gifted seventeen-year-old, a star athlete, captain of the basketball team, a professional surfer, risk himself like that? On stage, by the podium, the answer I was looking for dawned on me. I collapsed because it was too much. I couldn't believe that I… I was the one guilty of your crash.

"I blacked out and was transported to the hospital. I don't remember anything. The security guard didn't randomly toss that comment at me. You were there that night, in the lab. You probably hid somewhere so you could startle me like we always used to do to each other. You probably waited patiently for the right opportunity, you probably came to the lab to tell me about your victory, but instead, heard what you shouldn't have heard. You were probably horrified, you felt cheated, angry, and unable to process it. And I understand, you were probably so mad. You wanted to do something, something extreme. Maybe you didn't care so much about your life in those moments, to the point that you were willing to risk it all. This may come as a surprise, but I do get you," Dad said solemnly and placed his hand on mine.

"Sometimes, I think of what might have happened if only you had lifted your head or made a little noise. If only I would have found out that you were in the lab all along, things could have ended differently... I'm sure of it." Dad's voice was hoarse and full of sorrow.

He ruffled his hair, got up, paced around the room, stared out the window, and returned to the seat by my bed.

"They told me I'd suffered a heart attack. But I didn't care too much. I tore out the infusion and, wearing the hospital gown, went outside and took a taxi straight to the lab. When I arrived, I entered the building's management room and asked to see the security camera videos. They were obviously a bit freaked out by my appearance, but they agreed anyway. A long hour later, they gave me the tape from the archive, and there you were. You were filmed walking with your bag to the entrance, locking your bike on the rack outside, and entering the building. There was nothing more to say, I didn't need to search anymore. I just sat there, replaying the tape over and over again, staring at you, struggling to grasp the truth. If only I had known, I could've turned things around," Dad said in desperation.

"It's important that you hear this. I didn't think of telling you about it because I'm your dad, I'm the one who raised you all these years. Who cares who your biological father is? It's just a technical matter. That's how I saw it all these years. You might think differently, but the moment you were born, the moment you entered my life, that was it, I became your father, no questions asked. I understand your anger, maybe our decision to keep this hidden from you seems extreme, but in any case, I'm here, telling you all of this, pleading for forgiveness, hoping you can forgive me. If you can hear me, I'm here, I'm sorry, so sorry." Dad stroked my face and smiled.

"That's it, that's all I wanted to say." He got up from his chair, kissed me on the forehead, gazed at me for a few minutes, and then, finally, left the room.

Several minutes later, the medical staff and my parents returned. Mom and Dad stood by the window again as the nurses surrounded my bed and the doctor perched himself above me. The moment of truth had come, there was nowhere to run.

Mom approached the bed and kissed me on the forehead repeatedly. "This is goodbye," she grieved. I remember her telling me something, but I couldn't really hear, everything began to grow dim and blurry. While I was physically present in the room, I was no longer really with them. The voices returned with all their force to pull me in. This time, I didn't object. I felt like I was ready to let go, move forward, and follow them wherever. I was giving up. They surrounded me from all sides, and I surrendered to them. The little energy I had left vanished, dissolved. I felt like I was sinking deeper into another world. Even though I was afraid, I felt a pleasant sense of relief.

"Am I dead or alive?" I remember asking myself, still able to see Mom and Dad's sad expressions as they watched the medical staff. I began to sink deeper.

The staff finished what they came to do, and Mom and Dad leaned in for a final goodbye. Dad stretched out his trembling hand and grabbed mine. At that moment, I knew I owed him my forgiveness. I remember saying in my heart, "I forgive you." I wish I could move my finger, just to let him know I'm here, that I truly forgive him, I told myself, feeling desperate. But it was too late, there was no point in wishing for irrational things to happen.

Despite it all, I didn't feel lonely. My bro was with me, I was happy, really happy. I felt calm having him with me. I felt safe and prepared for what was yet to come. If there was one reasonable thing to come out of this, it was Him. Knowing that He was with me, always. It gave me so much strength. I made peace with the voices that pushed me to the world beyond. I understood that it was my time to go. It was the first time I truly felt ready to say goodbye, I no longer fought back. That's it, I let go. I waited, like the rest of the people in the room, for the fatal dose that would put an end to it all. And then it happened...

Suddenly, I felt a surge of power, and miraculously, I was able to move my finger a bit upward. "Am I imagining things, or is this real?" I asked myself utterly confused. My brain gave another order to my finger to move, and again it obeyed and slightly twitched. I couldn't believe it. In that instant, all the voices fell silent, as if all of their immense power had been sapped, and waited along with me, in complete suspense, to see if anyone else had seen my finger's subtle movement.

"It moved! His finger moved!" my dad cried out in shock and shoved the doctor aside.

"Look!" he yelled, and my mom rushed quickly to the bed.

"What's going on?" she cried in surprise and wiped her tears.

"Stop! Stop everything!" Dad burst out.

At that moment, I knew it was happening! It was really happening! Time froze, and it was like I was no longer there, but back in the room with everyone.

"What's happening?" I asked my bro, confused. But there was no need to wait for an answer, I understood very well. I had forgiven my father, and my miracle came through.

"Are you here?" my dad asked.

I blinked my eyes in response.

"Unbelievable!" my dad declared and pulled me closer, practically ripping me off the bed.

My mom hugged the two of us tightly, her warm tears rubbing onto my face. It was the first time since the surgery that I could actually feel something. My body was coming back to life. I could suddenly feel the heat of their bodies and their trembling hands. I felt the warmth of their salty tears dripping on my body. It was incredible. I really couldn't believe this was happening.

ONE YEAR LATER

15.

I'm alive again.

Yeah, I'm back... who would've thought.

We're now on the summit of the mountain, taking in the incredible view spread below us. The air here is thin, so thin we can barely breathe, but it's well worth it. All the effort we put in, all those long days climbing up the hills, just so we could reach this snowy peak, it's all worth it.

"I'm free!" I yelled with all my force, feeling freer than ever. So many things have happened this past year, but only here, on the summit of this snowy mountain in faraway Nepal, do I realize how free I am. I'm not the same boy who was trapped in his paralyzed body.

Today, I admire every muscle, nerve, and every wink my body does. I returned to my normal life after long months of intense rehabilitation.

At first, I could do nothing more than move my fingers, blink, and move my lips. A week later, my whole body began to move, until I could finally sit upright and talk. The medical crew in the vegetative department I was hospitalized in for years deemed my case "a medical miracle."

During my first days awake, tens of doctors and nurses from all departments of the hospital came to see "the miracle child" with their own eyes, the boy who returned from the dead.

Apparently, several doctors were researching this very topic, and it was important for them to understand what really happened to me, where I was all these years, and what caused my sudden return. They asked me a bunch of questions and wrote down every single detail in their thick files. I found it all a bit funny. I tried to explain to them what happened, how I agreed to forgive, how this was all a miracle, and that my bro prepared me for this miracle way before it even happened, but it seemed like my stories didn't really interest them. All they were interested in was my physical state. They wanted data, before and after brain scans. I don't get them, they weren't willing to listen to me. I tried to explain, but it was useless.

When it comes to my friends, I've long since become their usual joke. They laugh at me endlessly and at every opportunity. Every time we meet up, all it takes is one small remark and that's it, everyone's on fire, tossing their usual jokes about me in the air.

"So, Yair, while all of us worked our asses off in the army, you hung around in the hospital, right? Tell us the truth," someone says, and immediately everyone cracks up.

They're unstoppable, these guys. They live for it.

"So, Yair, one little syringe is enough to scare you back to life?" And everyone laughs.

"Look at Yair, he could've woken up years ago..." Someone pokes me with a plastic syringe and everyone rolls on the floor laughing.

"The guy dropped almost one hundred feet into the

ditch, lay for five years in the hospital with a broken body, but noooo, don't get anywhere near him with a syringe. Just don't stab him, you hear? Just not with a syringe... anything but the syringe."

There's also the funny imitation of the nurse with the heavy Hungarian accent, which, God knows where that came from. "Yair, my sweet child... no need to be afraid of syringe... no need. One little stab... just one, my dear boy." Every time the heavy accent comes up, everyone explodes into a fit of laughter. It's crazy how much I missed these idiots.

Honestly, it's good to be back. I'm happy to be with everyone, even though I can see them look at me at times like I'm a zombie who came back from the dead. I don't blame them; it really is hard to fathom where I was before waking up, and what exactly happened to me these past five years. In some sense, I feel like I owe an explanation to those around me, where I've been, and what really went down. That's why I wrote this book about my journey, to help them understand what happened to me, because my time in the hospital wasn't spent lying around lifelessly. On the contrary, a lot happened to me, things that wouldn't have happened in our normal reality.

The moment I got out of the hospital, I knew I'd write this book. I knew I had some sort of mission now, that I didn't come back from the dead for no reason. The miracle that happened to me turned my life around. And I now know how huge it is that I'm here, healthy and alive, and not there, dead in the afterworld. The miracle that happened to me is unbelievable.

I remind myself every day how lucky I am that I returned, and how easily I could've been in the world above us, stuck at the bottom of the pyramid.

I feel like I need to dedicate this book to the one who

helped me, who was there for me, who accompanied me, who never gave up on me, and without who I wouldn't be here today, my bro.

Regarding the trip to Nepal, I didn't go with a friend, nor with Talila, but with my dad, and we're more than glad about it. My dad has completely changed since the crash. He's not the same dad from before.

In the early mornings, as I write, he reads and waits for me to finish. At noon, we normally get walking, on to our next destination. He doesn't ask me what I write about, but I believe he knows. He understands that I've been through major things these past years and that I have to pass them on, write them on paper, for the readers to know.

The best thing that has happened to me since the crash is that I began talking with my bro, who is with me everywhere and at all times. Both when I was there, and now that I'm back here.

If I could ask my readers for one thing only, it would be for them to talk with Him too. Just talk. He's not far away, He's really close, open to talking with each and every one of you.

I needed to get to the lowest and darkest of places just so I could find Him. But you don't have to get there. You can start talking to Him now, each day, for a couple of minutes. Don't make it too complicated, just make room for Him.

Made in United States
North Haven, CT
05 January 2024